"How often does a storm like this hit?"

"Only once in the five years since I had the house built. That time it blew in the windows, but it was stronger."

Hence his brusque instruction to steer clear of them. "The hotel made no mention of anything."

"It developed without warning," Nick said. "It happens."

Much like his recent effect on me, I thought darkly, watching him shove his hands through his hair as he continued to glare at the floor and pace, about as removed from cool, in control and immaculate as it was possible to be.

"How long do they last?" I asked, deciding it would be wise to focus on the practicalities instead of my intensely confusing and unwelcome response to him.

"If we're lucky, it'll be over in a matter of hours. If we aren't, it could be days."

Days?

God.

"So what do we do in the meantime?"

He paused midstep and shot me a look that was as dark and stormy as the sky. Something in it ignited a fire in the pit of my stomach and sent heat streaking along my veins.

Lucy King spent her adolescence lost in the glamorous and exciting world of Harlequin when she really ought to have been paying attention to her teachers. But as she couldn't live in a dreamworld forever, she eventually acquired a degree in languages and an eclectic collection of jobs. After a decade in southwest Spain, Lucy now lives with her young family in Wiltshire, England. When not writing or trying to think up new and innovative things to do with mince, she spends her time reading, failing to finish cryptic crosswords and dreaming of the golden beaches of Andalucia.

Books by Lucy King

Harlequin Presents

Passionately Ever After...
Undone by Her Ultra-Rich Boss

Passion in Paradise
A Scandal Made in London

Lost Sons of Argentina
The Secrets She Must Tell
Invitation from the Venetian Billionaire
The Billionaire without Rules

Visit the Author Profile page
at Harlequin.com for more titles.

Lucy King

STRANDED WITH MY FORBIDDEN BILLIONAIRE

Recycling programs
for this product may
not exist in your area.

ISBN-13: 978-1-335-73900-1

Stranded with My Forbidden Billionaire

Copyright © 2022 by Lucy King

For questions and comments about the quality of this book,
please contact us at CustomerService@Harlequin.com.

Harlequin Enterprises ULC
22 Adelaide St. West, 41st Floor
Toronto, Ontario M5H 4E3, Canada
www.Harlequin.com

Printed in U.S.A.

STRANDED WITH MY FORBIDDEN BILLIONAIRE

CHAPTER ONE

IF SOMEONE HAD told me six weeks ago that, come November, I'd be aboard a speedboat jetting towards Nick Morgan's private island in the Indian Ocean, five thousand miles from my flat share in London, with the intention of requesting his help, I'd have stared at them in astonishment and asked what they were on.

For the sake of my older brother, Seb, with whom he'd been friends for years, Nick and I were just about civil to each other whenever our paths crossed, but we didn't get along.

We'd met when he'd started at our exclusive boarding school in the same year as my brother. They were both thirteen and I was eleven. Seb and I were the children of a multimillionaire financier who had single-handedly funded the school's new business studies centre. Nick was the clever son of a single mother, who had grown up in poverty and been awarded a free place. He found me impossibly spoilt and shallow, I knew, while I considered him absurdly aloof and uptight.

Since then, our fortunes had dramatically reversed but things between us were still as frosty as ever and, under normal circumstances, hell would have to freeze over before I'd ever seek him out.

But then I won one hundred and eight million pounds on the national lottery—give or take a penny or two—and was very nearly scammed out of half of it, and that changed everything.

'You need proper professional help, Millie,' Seb told me when I rang him in a panic, my heart pounding and my palms sweating as the delayed shock of the win, the near miss I'd had with the fraudsters and the realisation of how suddenly vulnerable I was on so many fronts finally hit home. 'Get in touch with Nick. He does this sort of thing for a living and he's extremely good at it.'

Seb was right. Over the last decade, Nick had made a fortune from dishing out top-level financial advice and the sales of products he'd developed off the back of it. He'd started his career as an advocate of the high risk, high reward way of making money on someone else's payroll before switching to a slower, steadier approach to wealth management when he set up on his own. He'd developed an unshakeable reputation for both ability and trustworthiness and, grudgingly, I had to admit that if anyone was the man for the job, it was probably him.

There was just one teeny tiny problem.

'Nick hates me,' I said, recalling with a shiver the hard set of his jaw and the chill that appeared in his slate-grey gaze whenever he laid eyes on me these days.

'He doesn't.'

'He does.'

'Either way,' said Seb, clearly reluctant to venture down that rabbit hole yet again, 'how is that relevant?'

'It might make him less inclined to help.'

'I very much doubt that. The fees he'd earn would be astronomical. He won't be able to resist.'

'But he already has billions,' I said, all too easily able to envisage a scenario where he coolly heard me out and then baldly refused, as if trying to make some kind of a point, to mete out an unnecessary lesson in humility, perhaps. 'Is he that driven by money?'

'He's *only* driven by money,' came the dry reply down the line from San Francisco. 'But seriously, Mills, he'll take care of you. He's the man you need. Believe me.'

I didn't need any man, least of all one who loathed me, nor did I want to be taken care of. When our father lost everything virtually overnight eight years ago, a month before my twenty-first birthday, I'd crash-landed in the real world. Among other things, I'd learned the importance of self-reliance and the value of independence, and now fiercely guarded both. And while men were fine for the rare occasion I fancied a spot of company on a cold night, the only proper boyfriend I'd ever had had unceremoniously dumped me the minute I became penniless. The experience had been crushing and I wasn't keen to repeat it.

But one hundred and eight million pounds was a mammoth responsibility. I knew nothing of investments other than that as well as up, they could go down, down and down some more, and my brush with the scammers suggested I might possibly have inherited my father's rash decision-making when it came to handling a fortune. I did need help, I had to admit. And, with Seb's suggestion flashing like a beacon in my head and the unsolicited offers of advice from people I'd never heard of still coming in thick and fast, I'd eventually thought, *better the devil you know.*

So I'd emailed Nick, who informed me that if I wanted to see him I'd have to hop on a plane, and now here I was twenty-four hours later, half-way around the world, part furious that I was so desperate for his help I'd had to acquiesce to his summons, part relieved he hadn't simply told me to get lost.

As the boat I'd picked up in Dar es Salaam sped across the sparkling sapphire water with James, the driver that came with it, at the helm, the small land mass shimmering on the horizon grew and solidified. I shaded my eyes against the bright sun that blazed in a cloudless sky and, in an attempt to distract myself from the nerves that were twisting my stomach because I had no idea of the reception I was going to get, focused on the scenery.

The glorious stretch of curving white sand beach fringed with palm trees that hove into view was like something out of a glossy brochure. It was perfect, alluring, and so mesmerising I barely noticed the water turning to a light jade in colour as it shallowed, or the boat gradually slowing. It was only when we bumped against something solid, jolting me out of my trance, that I whipped my head round to find out what was going on and realised with a quick skip of my pulse that we'd arrived and I had a welcome party.

Of one.

Nick.

Who was standing on the gently bobbing pontoon with his arms folded across his broad chest and looking at me with his habitual inscrutability.

His face was set, his eyes were dark and his

jaw was rigid, but that was where the familiarity ended, I noticed, my mouth drying and my skin prickling in a most peculiar way as I took in the rest of his appearance. His usually immaculate hair was longer than normal, and ruffled. Instead of his customary tailor-made suit, he had on a pair of turquoise board shorts, patterned, no less, with a multicoloured tropical plant print. In place of the inevitable pristine white shirt that he always wore with the two top buttons undone was, of all astonishing things, a lemon-yellow polo shirt.

What was going on? I wondered, baffled and not a little unsettled by the unexpected sight of some toned tanned biceps and a pair of long, surprisingly muscled legs. So much colour. Such informality. Could he be ill? And where, in all that was holy, were his *shoes*?

'Nick, hi,' I said, parking these bewildering questions for later analysis and plastering on a bright smile while deciding to attribute the jitters bouncing around inside me to the long overnight flight.

'A pleasure to see you as always, Amelia,' he replied as he deftly caught the rope that James cast in his direction, and pulled it taut.

Despite the distracting flurry of activity and the impressive flexing of muscles, I tensed minutely and inwardly winced at the lie. At any lie, in fact. The closest, most important relationship of my youth—the one I'd had with my father—had turned out to be the biggest lie of all and these days I valued honesty, no matter how brutal.

So I didn't reply with a socially conventional but meaningless 'likewise'. But nor did I react to Nick's use of my full name with my usual roll of the eyes, because at thirty thousand feet above Egypt I'd come up with a simple yet mature strategy for this meeting.

One, ignore the past and focus on the present.

Two, keep things professional at all times.

And finally, perhaps most importantly, stay calm and resist the temptation to respond to Nick's dislike of me by instinctively exhibiting the silliness and superficiality he expected, in a sort of sticking two fingers up at him kind of a way.

Instead, I breathed in through my mouth and out through my nose, deeply and slowly and repeatedly, until the sulky teen in me had flounced off and I was channelling Zen-like serenity.

'Thank you,' I said smoothly, accepting the hand he held out and stepping off the boat and onto the pontoon.

He let me go abruptly and frowned down at the huge suitcase James was struggling to lift up and out. 'How long are you planning on staying?'

'Not long,' I said, surreptitiously rubbing my

hand against my skirt in an attempt to dispel the strange tingling sensation that lingered while Nick relieved James of his burden as if it weighed no more than a feather.

'It feels like you've packed for weeks.'

'Just a fortnight.'

He shot me a look, a flicker of alarm breaking through the ice-cool reserve, which meant he had to be seriously rattled by the idea. 'A fortnight?'

'Don't worry,' I assured him as he tossed the rope back to James. 'I don't intend to spend it here.'

Perish the thought. I knew when I wasn't wanted. And it was fine. I was well used to being on my own, and actually, I preferred things like that. Experience had taught me relationships weren't to be trusted. I'd learnt the hard way how fickle other people could be, when those I'd considered my friends, including my then boyfriend, had ghosted me at a time I'd needed them most.

I couldn't even rely on family, I'd eventually come to realise. My father, whom I'd adored, had emotionally distanced himself the minute he'd discovered my mother was having an affair with her personal trainer and had decided to redirect all his efforts into winning her back. Thanks to my role in the breakdown of their marriage in the first place, my mother and I had a tricky relationship at the best of times, and my brother, the only person I might have been able to count on, lived five thousand miles and eight time zones away so was therefore more often out of reach than he was in it.

But none of that was anything new. I'd accepted it and adapted to it years ago. And if the self-reliance and the tough outer shell I'd developed meant that I allowed no one to get close, that I had no one to talk to about my hopes and fears, or anyone with whom to share my tumultuous and conflicted feelings about my lottery win, well, the occasional pang of loneliness was a small price to pay for self-preservation. True friendship, love of the romantic kind, marriage in particular, required a level of trust I simply couldn't see myself ever embracing. Emotional involvement in anything only led to confusion, pain and heartbreak. It was far easier, far *safer*, for me and for others, if I steered well clear of all of it.

'I wasn't aware I'd invited you to,' said Nick, his tersely made point snapping me out of my ruminations and obliterating the twinges of regret I nevertheless felt at the way things had turned out.

No, well, quite, I thought, determinedly pulling myself together. And thank goodness for it. Days of stilted conversation and keeping out of each other's way? The tension and awkwardness would be unbearable and very much *not* my idea of a good time. 'I've booked myself a room at a hotel on Zanzibar.'

At the *best* hotel on Zanzibar, in actual fact. Where, according to its website, Scandi minimalism met hints of the Middle East amidst twenty hectares of lush tropical gardens. Where, for my first holiday abroad in eight years, two weeks of pampering and indulgence awaited me, along with a waterfall bar, two infinity pools and a villa that came with a dedicated butler. Instead of schlepping to and from the office where I worked as a manager in the dark November mizzle, I'd be sliding on my sunglasses and trotting to my sun lounger with a book. There'd be long, blissful naps and lazy, luxurious massages. Yoga for breakfast and lobster for dinner, and, with any luck, a tan.

Just like old times.

Well, not *quite* like old times, perhaps. Old times would have also involved diving with my dad, the two of us gliding among the fish and the coral in the silky silence thirty feet beneath the surface of warm turquoise water, the connection and trust between us stronger than steel. Or so I'd always imagined, until amidst the wreckage of our misfortune I'd discovered that he wasn't the hero I'd believed him to be, that the unique bond I'd thought we shared was nothing more than an illusion, that I didn't actually know him at all…

But still.

I could hardly wait.

'The helicopter's coming to pick me up in an hour,' I told Nick, shaking off the conflicting emotions of grief and loss, pain and betrayal that could still blindside me, even now, seven years, six months and twenty-one days after my father's fatal heart attack, and dragging myself back to the present.

'Good,' he said flatly. 'The quicker we sort out what you want from me and you go on your way, the better.'

He turned to stride back up the pontoon, my suitcase in his hand, while I stood there waving James off, his words ringing in my ears, suddenly feeling a little dazed, a little winded, and thinking that perhaps, on reflection, brutal honesty wasn't quite all it was cracked up to be.

CHAPTER TWO

IT WAS A five-minute walk along a sandy path that cut through dense verdant vegetation to reach Nick's house, which gave me ample opportunity to reflect upon my bizarre response to the feel of his hand around mine and the quick tightening of my chest at his parting shot.

The former was easy enough to explain. Despite having known each other for eighteen years, Nick and I had never actually touched. Not once. Which was odd when I'd always been the touchy-feely sort. But as a surly teenager, he'd radiated back-off vibes, and in the years following my sixteenth birthday pool party at which I'd irretrievably shattered all possibility of a friendly sort of relationship, any contact would have resulted in frostbite.

These days, whenever we met—mostly on the occasions my brother was over from the States and arranged a get-together—we tended to give each other a cool sort of nod and a very wide berth. So it was little wonder that actual frostbite-free physical contact, however fleeting, would come as a shock so intense I could still feel it zinging through me.

The sense of being thumped in the solar plexus at the implication that he couldn't wait for me to leave was harder to fathom. It suggested that I cared about what he thought of me, but that wasn't the case. I truly didn't. His continued brooding yet unspoken disapproval of my superficiality—once undoubtedly justified—was unwarranted these days, and if he couldn't move on and accept that I was no longer an over-indulged, self-absorbed teenager then that was his problem, not mine.

Maybe it stung because up until that moment he'd never openly expressed his dislike of me, and to have it confirmed somehow made it unequivo-cally real. Or maybe, with the stress I'd been under recently and the lack of a support network, which I'd been feeling more acutely than usual, I was simply more sensitive to a barb that otherwise might have bounced right off, and overreacting. Who knew? And what did it matter? Ultimately, all that was important was securing Nick's help in managing the fortune that had dropped into my lap and already caused so much trouble.

The shrubbery thinned and the path came to an end, along with my ruminations, which were flat-tened by the impact of the sight that met my eyes.

Built from wood painted a blinding white and possessing innumerable windows and glass doors off which the sun glinted, the two-storey villa was vast and stunning. Tall pillars on the ground floor supported a veranda that wrapped around the first, providing the long wide terrace below with dappled shade. The enormous raised rectangular pool had clear sides so the water within looked like a thick solid slab of cobalt. A vast swathe of emerald-green grass edged the beach, beyond which lay the sparkling sea. Palm trees swished in the breeze and brightly coloured flowers stood in planters dotted around the grounds. As tropical paradises went this one was unbeatable, and I'd seen a few.

'This is a lovely house,' I said with what had to be the understatement of the century as I hauled my jaw off the floor and followed him up the wide timber steps to the deck.

'I like it.'

'I can see why you choose to spend the winters here.'

'I'm not a fan of the cold.'

'Oh, I don't know,' I said, acutely aware that sweat was about to start trickling unattractively down my temples, although why the attractiveness of anything should matter I had no idea. 'Hot chocolate, roaring fires and cashmere. What's not to like?'

'Winter isn't hot chocolate, roaring fires and cashmere for everyone,' he said in a tone that shrivelled my stomach and sent a flush to my cheeks that had nothing to do with the heat.

No. Right. Stupid of me. Nick had grown up with very little. I remembered my brother telling me once years ago when I must have been about thirteen that his mother had frequently had to make the choice between eating and heating. Unable to comprehend such a situation and, in all honesty, not particularly interested in my brother's lanky taciturn friend anyway, I'd shrugged and put it from my mind, one of the many moments of which I'm not proud.

'I guess not,' I said, berating myself for yet again speaking without thinking, which unfortunately happened all too often in his vicinity, and pushing aside the shame of the past to focus on the present. 'I've heard cashmere attracts moths anyway.'

With one quick disbelieving glance in my direction, Nick strode through a pair of open French doors into a bright, airy kitchen that was the size of the poky flat in zone four I shared with two others, dumped my suitcase and then headed for a run of glossy wood units that stretched across the width of the far end of the room.

'Would you like a drink?'

God, yes, I thought wistfully as I set my handbag down on the enormous bleached-wood-topped island and perched on a stool. A large rosemary-garnished gin and tonic—something to settle the jitters and quench my thirst—would be heavenly. But it wasn't even midday and I didn't need another black mark against me, especially when I so badly needed his help. 'A coffee would be great, thanks.'

He turned to a machine that was all buttons and spouts and looked as though it could orbit the earth, and while it hissed and burbled, I took the opportunity to study him.

No doubt this casual look of his was such a surprise because whenever we did meet these days he clearly came straight from work and it was hard to imagine him in anything other than a suit. And equally obviously, it was because we were always in the company of others, my attention diverted, that I'd never before noticed the breadth of his shoulders beneath the fine wool or the corded muscles of his forearms that appeared when, having taken off his jacket, he inevitably rolled up the sleeves of his shirt.

I'd certainly never seen him doing anything as pedestrian as stirring a spoonful of sugar into a macchiato, I mused, my gaze narrowing in on the action. It was strange how fascinating his economy of movement was, how mesmerising his hands were. If the touch of his palm against mine could send a sizzle of electricity shooting up my arm, what effect might it have on other parts of my body? Such as my waist…my thighs…my breasts…?

A shocking image of him abandoning the machine and spinning round to haul me into a crushing embrace slammed into my head then and I instantly went hot. My mouth dried. My lungs froze. My pulse gave a great kick and then started racing.

What was going on? I wondered, frantically scrubbing the all too vivid vision from my mind and struggling for control. Why was I even *thinking* of his hands on me? I hadn't before. A clinch of any kind, crushing or otherwise, had never crossed my mind. Well, not for years, at least. So why now?

Objectively, I could see he was exceptionally good-looking. He'd grown out of his lankiness years ago, and at well over six foot, with a broad, lean physique and a harshly beautiful face composed of strong, masculine features, he was the epitome of tall, dark and handsome. And judging by the way he had a different woman on his arm in every photo I'd ever seen him in, I wasn't the only one to know that.

But this was *Nick*. Impossibly and eternally uptight, judgemental and disapproving, and therefore very much *not* my type any more.

'Here you go,' he said, and I jumped, rattled by the lurid waywardness of my thoughts. He slid the cup of hot strong deliciousness in my direction, and frowned. 'Are you all right?'

No. I wasn't all right at all. I'd clearly lost my mind. But I had to get a grip, because he was as sharp as a knife and if he somehow managed to figure out what was going on in my head... It didn't bear thinking about.

'I'm fine,' I said, somehow managing to drum up a breezy smile while inwardly pulling myself together and outwardly fanning my face. 'I'm just not used to this heat. And it's been a hectic twenty-four hours.'

'You must be desperate to have flown all this way so quickly.'

He had no idea. For a moment I wondered if he took pleasure from having me dangling from his strings, but, quite frankly, I doubted he took plea-sure in anything. I'd certainly never heard or seen any evidence of it. Naturally I hadn't paid those photos all that much attention, but even when in the company of a stunning blonde he seemed to exude cool indifference.

'I am,' I said, taking the cup and belatedly thinking I should have asked for my coffee to be iced since yet more heat sliding through my body could well lead to combustion. 'I got your email and caught the next available flight.'

'I'm flattered.'

'You didn't leave me much choice.'

Not that it had been that much of a hardship, once I'd got over my indignation at being summonsed so high-handedly. I'd decided to fly first class, which had been as comfortable as I remembered. The lounge. The personal service. The comfort, the quiet and the champagne you didn't have to pay extra for. Everything I'd once taken for granted, I'd realised on the occasion I'd flown to Scotland with a no-frills airline, although, actually, none of it got you to your destination any faster.

Of course, the experience had cost a lot—even more once I'd guiltily paid extra to offset the increased carbon footprint flying first class generated—but I didn't need to worry about that now. Financially, I didn't need to worry about anything ever again, as long as I stayed away from scoundrels out to fleece me. And no doubt once that properly sank in, I'd be thrilled and excited and over the moon with happiness instead of anxious and nauseous and, at times, downright petrified.

'But thank you for agreeing to see me,' I added, recalling my intention to remain professional and in control and, above all, mature. 'You're bound to be busy and I realise that my coming here must be very inconvenient.'

'Perhaps you should tell me what you want from me,' he said, leaning back against the counter and folding his arms across his formidable chest in a move that for a second made my mouth dry and my heartbeat flutter. 'Before your helicopter gets here.' He glanced at his watch. 'Time is marching.'

Yes. Good plan. Enough of this pulse-skipping nonsense and bizarre disappointment that he hadn't contradicted my allegations of his busyness and my inconvenience. I was here for one thing, and one thing only.

'Six weeks ago, I won one hundred and eight million pounds on the lottery,' I said, reminding myself sternly of what that one thing was, which was absolutely *not* a steamy embrace from a man who'd always despised me.

Nick's only response to my news was a minute arch of an eyebrow, but then presumably, unlike me these days, he was used to such vast sums. To him, the amount could quite possibly be small change. I, on the other hand, had nearly passed out when I'd learnt how much I'd won.

'That would buy a lot of handbags.'

I instinctively bristled at the barb, but heroically rose above it. 'Well, that would depend on the handbag,' I said coolly. 'But I have other plans for it.'

'Which are?'

'Currently a bit overwhelming. That's why I'm here. I need your help.'

He was silent for a moment, then tilted his head and said dryly, '*Now* you need my help?'

Ah, yes.

That.

It had occurred to me he might bring it up. It was one of the reasons I hadn't contacted him for advice the minute I'd got over the shock of winning—apparently there was no statute of limitations on shame.

Shortly after the freezing of my father's assets, which had meant the repossession of my London penthouse, the abrupt mid-course end to my university studies in Zurich and the cutting off of my five-figure monthly allowance, Nick, sprinting his way up the ladder of the financial institution he'd joined on leaving Cambridge, had offered me a loan. A large one. Distraught, humiliated and an emotional wreck after everything that had happened, I'd flippantly flung his money back in his face, convinced that he was rubbing my nose into his success and my misfortune. He'd taken it badly, judging by the way he hadn't allowed me to apologise for the manner in which I'd refused him, hence the continued frostiness.

'I'm not unaware of the irony,' I said, shifting awkwardly on the stool while my cheeks warmed.

'What took you so long?'

'I thought I could manage,' I admitted with a frown. 'But the sharks started circling and I came to think otherwise.'

'What happened?'

'I nearly bought a tropical island that didn't exist.'

'I'm not surprised.'

Ooh, ouch. 'I know,' I said, ignoring the sting I felt pierce my chest like the pointiest of darts. I'd been a fool, and it annoyed me beyond belief because I thought I'd shed the innocence and naïveté of my youth years ago. 'Silly me, right?'

'Lottery winners are exceptionally vulnerable to fraud, in my experience. The shock tends to destroy logic.'

'You can say that again,' I muttered. 'I haven't been thinking straight in weeks.'

'Didn't anyone from the organisation tell you that you should do nothing until you've had some advice?'

'Yes,' I said with a sigh, unable to summon up much despair at the censure I could hear in his voice since it was wholly justified. 'They did. And

I got advice. Just the wrong kind. I'd requested anonymity—and told nobody outside the organisation apart from my mother and my brother—but I was nevertheless bombarded with offers of help. It didn't occur to me that the news must have got out anyway and that some of those offers would be less than genuine. I know it should have.'

'What stopped you going through with it?'

'Seb,' I said, my mind reeling back to the moment I realised that I might be being taken for a fool and tens of millions of dollars. The plummeting of my stomach. The nausea rising up my throat. The cataclysmic shock and the blind panic. 'He said if it sounded too good to be true it probably was. I sent him the details and he did the digging I should have done and discovered it was a sham.'

'You're lucky to have him.'

'I am,' I said with a nod. 'He was the one who suggested I contact you. I should have done it weeks ago. I know you're the best at what you do.'

'So why didn't you?'

'I guess I just didn't think you'd be prepared to help.'

'Why not?'

I stared at him for a second, momentarily lost for words. Did he really not know? Surely he couldn't be oblivious to the tension that throbbed between us, the strange sort of antagonism that developed whenever we came within six feet of each other, or the turbulent history we shared. Surely it couldn't all be a figment of my imagination? 'Well, we're not exactly friends, are we?'

His brow creased, a tiny frown that was gone in a flash that suggested I could have put it a little less bluntly. 'That's irrelevant.'

'How so?'

'I never let the personal get in the way of the professional.'

'Then you'll help?' I said, thinking it was a relief to know we were on the same page when it came to that, at least, and mentally crossing my fingers.

He gave a short nod. 'I'll help.'

CHAPTER THREE

So Seb had been right, I thought, noting the determined set of Nick's jaw and the glint of resolve—and possibly pound signs—in his eyes. He *was* willing to put profit above clearly uncomfortable personal feelings and petty point scoring. Or maybe he felt he owed my family something. Payback for the weekends and holidays he'd once spent with us, perhaps. Whatever his motives, he was prepared to help, and thank God for it because up until this very moment I'd had no idea how truly stressed and overwhelmed I'd been by everything.

Recently, my hard-won self-reliance hadn't felt like a strength. A noose round my neck would be a better description. Since the win, many had been the night I'd stared up at the ceiling riddled with anxiety, wishing I found it easier to trust in others and regretting that I couldn't let people get close. One hundred and eight million pounds was an inconceivable, terrifying amount, and I'd had no one nearby to even talk to about it.

Until now.

Now I had the most unlikely of knights in shining armour, I realised, my defences fracturing at the knowledge I wasn't in this alone any more. Nick would take care of my fortune. He wouldn't rip me off. He had more than enough money of his own. On this, at least, I could trust him, I was sure, and the relief that then flooded my system was so profound, so immense it was almost palpable. The tightness in my muscles vanished. The tight knots in my stomach dissolved, and the tumultuous emotions I'd been keeping such a tight lid on lately—shock, worry, excitement, fear, to name but a few—burst free, buffeting me on all sides with a ferocity that whipped the breath from my lungs and blitzed my mind.

Beneath the onslaught, my heart pounded, my mouth dried and my limbs turned to water. The hand I pressed weakly to my chest trembled. My self-control was fast becoming history. I was seconds away from disintegrating into a sobbing grateful heap in front of a man who already thought me a superficial naïve fool, and alarmingly, distressingly, there seemed to be nothing I could do about it.

Until Nick's voice cut through the fog and the madness.

'Are you about to start crying?'

The horror I heard in his tone stopped the whirling of my thoughts and the emotional battering of my nerves in their tracks. Reeling back from the brink of collapse, I blinked rapidly and swallowed down the painful lump lodged in my throat. I took a deep breath and as my head cleared of the dizziness I straightened my spine and got a grip of both my teeming emotions and my still warm cup.

'No, no,' I said, taking a quick sip of coffee to disguise my distress and somehow managing to sound more or less normal. 'Of course not.'

'Are you sure?'

'Absolutely.'

It had been a close call but, thanks to Nick very much not being the sort of man to offer me a shoulder to weep on, danger had been averted at the last minute. If ever there was a time for a brutal lack of sympathy, a second ago had been it, and for that I was grateful.

'Good.' He gave a brisk nod, all business now, which my still fragile composure appreciated. 'So what *do* you want to do with your money?'

This was better. Plans. Logistics. I could handle practicalities far more than I could deal with emotion right now, and I'd been considering the options for weeks.

'First, I'd like to buy a house,' I said, calling to mind the list I'd made with its many question marks, all caps and crossings out.

'You could buy a dozen houses.'

'I don't need a dozen,' I said. 'Just the one will do.'

'A three-storey mansion in Chelsea with a garage for a fleet of cars?'

A replica of the home in which I'd grown up? Was that a dig? I tilted my head and regarded him thoughtfully for a moment, but it was hard to tell. He was giving nothing away. And yet I didn't think I'd imagined the sardonic tinge to his words.

'I'm not sure a man who owns an island paradise in the Indian Ocean as well as penthouse apartments in half a dozen capital cities across the globe is in much of a position to judge,' I said, bristling a little.

'Who's judging?'

'You are. As usual.'

He frowned. 'As usual?'

'Yes.'

'I'll rephrase the question.'

'I'll save you the bother,' I replied, really not needing to be on the receiving end of another potentially barbed comment. 'I haven't decided what

I'd like to buy or where I'd like to live yet,' I said, only knowing that I didn't want to look back and recreate what I'd once had and lost, since it held few reliably happy memories and had all been built on sand anyway. 'But it will have space, a garden and no flatmates.'

'What else?'

'I'd like my mother to be provided for for the rest of her life.'

Nick's response to that was a sharp lift of his eyebrows and it triggered another stab of irritation. 'There you go again.'

'You're overreacting.'

'Next you'll be calling me hysterical.'

A glimmer of what looked like weary exasperation flickered across his face. 'I'm merely surprised.'

Yes, well, while his exasperation was rude and outrageous, his surprise I could understand. My mother and I had barely spoken since the funeral. Things between us were complicated and feelings ran deep. By monopolising my father's attention as a child, I'd inadvertently come between them. The jealousy and resentment she'd felt had led to her affair. Ultimately, I'd driven my parents apart and wrecked their marriage, so even though my mother had proved remarkably resilient in the face of adversity, dealing stoically with the aftermath of my father's fall from grace and then demise, ensuring her financial security was the least I could do. Would it assuage the guilt that still tormented me day in day out? I could only hope.

'We might not get along,' I said, having no intention of sharing anything so deeply personal with the annoyingly supercilious man before me, 'but she's still my mother.'

'I can draw up a few ideas.'

'That would be helpful.'

'What about Seb?'

'He's adamant he doesn't want any of it for himself,' I said, recalling the phone call in which I'd offered to transfer a lump sum to him and been turned down, which had unexpectedly hurt. 'But I know he's looking to expand his company. I thought I could maybe somehow help with that. Invest in it or something.'

On leaving university, Seb had moved to San Francisco to take up a job in Silicon Valley. A couple of years later he'd left to set up his own software business. The timing of the move could not have been worse. When they'd caught wind of our father's financial troubles, Seb's potential investors had jumped like rats off a sinking ship. If it hadn't been for Nick stepping in to provide the capital, he too might have wound up bankrupt.

'That could be an option,' said Nick with a short nod. 'What else?'

'What else would you advise?'

'A portfolio of short-, medium- and long-term investments.'

'All right,' I said, just about convincing myself that that would be wise. Who cared if it felt a bit dull? Dull was sensible and I was all about the sensible these days. 'I'm open to ideas. But nothing reckless.'

On the skids and veering further and further off the rails, my father had taken increasingly high risks in the hope of clawing back his mounting losses. The fallout had been catastrophic and a direct hit wasn't something I ever wanted to experience for myself.

'Nothing I do, either professionally or personally, is reckless.'

No, he was the most coolly controlled person I'd ever met. Sometimes it made me want to provoke and prod him just to see what might happen if he was pushed to his limits. That I'd always managed to resist was something of a miracle. 'I'm delighted to hear it.'

'Have you considered charitable donations?'

'I have a very long list. I'll email it to you.'

'Do you still have your job?'

'Yes.'

'Do you intend to keep it?'

'For the time being. If I can. Managing the office of a stationery company isn't exactly setting the world on fire, but it gave me purpose and structure at a time when I had none and I feel a certain degree of loyalty towards it. I get on well with my colleagues and right now it's the only thing in my life that's stable.'

'Were you serious about the island?'

Ah, yes, the island. A dream I'd had for God knew how many years, a dream that had been formed when diving with my father, that had inspired my degree in marine biology, and been dashed when overnight I'd had to leave university early and get a job that would slowly but surely pay off the six-figure debt on my credit card.

Once upon a time, I'd pored over maps and trawled through data. I'd compiled lists and calculated costings. There'd been nothing I hadn't known about endangered marine species and ecosystems. I'd filled a dozen archive boxes with my research and I'd hung onto them for months before eventually, reluctantly, heartbrokenly throwing them away.

'Very much so,' I said, thinking of the new folder I'd recently created on my laptop into which I was pouring ideas for everything I longed to achieve and was now within the realms

of possibility if I didn't screw it up, which unfortunately was entirely possible. 'I'm hoping to
set up some sort of marine conservation sanctuary. Bring in experts to build coral reefs and
implement breeding programmes. That sort of
thing. But I don't have the faintest idea how to
go about it.'

I half expected Nick to laugh at me, to tell me it
was way too ambitious a project for someone with
absolutely no experience—which was why I'd kept
my plans deliberately vague—but, 'I'll look into
it,' was all he said.

'Thank you,' I said with genuine gratitude,
the weight that had been crushing my chest for
weeks lifting so suddenly I felt as if I were floating. 'Don't forget to send me a contract.'

He frowned. 'A contract?'

'Your terms and conditions. Your fees.'

His jaw tightened in a curious way, as if I'd
offended him or something, which was bizarre.
'Sure,' he said with a strange twist of his mouth.
'Give me a week or so to put together a pro-
posal. I'll be in touch then. In the meantime,'
he added, pushing himself off the counter and
striding past me, pausing only to grab my suitcase as the whoop-whoop sound of an approach-
ing helicopter filled the space around us, 'here's
your ride.'

* * *

Seven days later, I was sitting at a table that over-looked the sparkling sea, replete after a platter of lobster followed by a fresh mango and papaya fruit salad. I took a sip of my postprandial limon-cello, then settled back to watch the jet skis criss-crossing the bay and the yachts drifting along the horizon against a backdrop of an azure sky dotted with fluffy white clouds.

As warm dreamy languor spread through me, I reflected that the best hotel on Zanzibar was exactly the experience I'd hoped for. It was ev-erything the website had promised, and more. The food—local, seasonal and mouth-wateringly spiced—was exquisite. My villa was the ultimate in luxurious comfort and I'd spent hours in the soothing tranquillity of the spa being pampered to within an inch of my life. I'd been diving each day and my tan was coming along nicely. With every minute that ticked lazily by, the stress and anxiety of the last couple of months faded that little bit more.

Of course, it might have been more fun to have a friend here to share it all with, and dining on my own meal after meal had begun to pall a little, but at least I could do what I wanted when I wanted and didn't have to worry about whether that friend was interested in me or my money. I knew well that possessing a fortune didn't come without its problems—especially with regards to other people's take on it—and everything was so much simpler without the whole poor little rich girl dynamic.

If I found the luxury and extravagance of my surroundings ever so slightly overwhelming, the bling of the well-heeled clientele over the top and not a little obscene, that was just because I wasn't used to them any more. Diving, with the conflicting feelings about my father that it triggered, would get easier with practice, I had no doubt, and soon I'd stop thinking about how much this was all costing and what else that money could buy, how much good it could do. I had more than enough to go round, and, now that Nick was on board, it was in safe hands.

Yesterday he'd sent me an email with his tenpage report. Over dinner, I'd scrolled through the tables, the figures and the recommendations with the intention of reading it more thoroughly this week, but it had struck me then that if I wanted to I could wash my hands of the details and know that my fortune would be well looked after. I didn't much like Nick's attitude towards me, but I'd always known where I stood with him. He'd never made any secret of the fact he found me lacking. He didn't mince his words or adopt a facade around me. I found his consistency on this, the absence of pretence, unexpectedly reassuring and I was certain that with my money, at least, I could trust him.

The buzz of my phone, which I'd silenced for lunch, jolted me out of my reverie. I put down my glass and picked it up. It was my brand-new financial advisor, no doubt calling to discuss his report. As a kick of adrenalin struck me in the stomach and a frisson of anticipation rippled down my spine I hit the green button and lifted the device to my ear. 'Hello?'

'Amelia,' said Nick, sounding even terser than usual. 'Are you all right?'

'I'm fine,' I said, slightly perplexed by the way his voice seemed to grate over my nerve-endings until I realised we'd never spoken on the phone before, which was undoubtedly why it felt so odd. 'Why wouldn't I be?'

'Have you been in touch with your family?'

'No. I haven't been in touch with anyone for days. What's wrong?'

'So you haven't seen the headlines?'

'What headlines?'

'Forget it,' he said, and cut the call.

For a moment I sat there staring at the phone in astonishment. What on earth had that been about? I'd never heard him so agitated. He'd sounded almost unhinged. But if he thought I was forgetting about anything after that, he could think again.

With my heart hammering like a steam train, I stared at the home screen, a powerful sense of misgiving sweeping through me. Was someone I loved hurt? What headlines could he be referring to? And why did I have seventy-eight unread emails in my inbox when an hour ago there'd been none?

Fifteen minutes later I had the answers to all the questions rocketing around my head, and a dozen more. Somehow, news of my lottery win had hit the papers. Under ordinary circumstances it might have merited a paragraph on perhaps page twelve, but the events of eight years earlier had elevated it to page one with links to opinion pieces and analysis.

It was all there. Everywhere. Rehashed photos of my hedonistic teenage years. Blistering commentary about privilege and responsibility and the frailty of human nature. Sycophantic messages from people I hadn't spoken to in years. Brutal reminders of a painful time.

And now, as if it had happened yesterday, memories slammed into my head one after the other like a thundering cascade. The shock I'd felt at the loss of money and status. Worse, the crucifying plunge of my father from the pedestal I'd put him on. The reassessment of everything in my life I'd believed to be true. The cruel mockery of strangers and the bewildering abandonment by so-called friends. The guilt, the humiliation, the fallout that had lasted far longer than the headlines.

This time round, in addition to raking over the past, there were also opinions on the unfairness of luck. Photos of the building where I lived now lay alongside the Chelsea mansion in which I'd grown up, with suitably catty captions. They'd even tracked down my work colleagues, who'd known nothing of my win, who wouldn't understand why I hadn't told them, who might well be hurt by the omission. None of them had commented yet, nor had either of my flatmates, but it was only a matter of time.

Just as it could only be a matter of time before the press found out where I was. How long did I have? If past experience was anything to go by it would be hours rather than days.

At the thought of what might be to come—the ridicule, the spite, the relentless pressure—the limoncello turned to battery acid in my stomach and the lobster and fruit revolted. Despite the warm breeze rustling through the palm trees, I couldn't breathe. My hands shook. Nausea rolled through me. Paradise had become poisonous.

Sweating, with panic tightening my throat and my heart beating too fast, I headed back to my room and rang first Seb and then, out of a weird kind of desperation, my mother, but both calls went to voicemail. I hung up, feeling achingly alone, hatefully pathetic, vulnerable and weak.

What was I going to do?

I couldn't stay here. It was doubtful I'd be recognised by any of the guests, but I was a sitting duck for a pap with a boat and a long-lensed camera. Yet if I left, where would I go? I couldn't go home. I'd be mobbed. And there was no one there for me anyway. Seb was on the other side of the world and why I'd called my estranged mother was beyond me.

I needed time to regroup and restore my defences. Somewhere safe. Secure. Where I'd be accommodated and protected, if not welcomed. Where at least if I was judged, I'd be expecting it.

I wasn't as alone as I felt, I reminded myself, a glimmer of light flickering in the darkness as I recalled the resolve with which Nick had told me he'd help with the management of my fortune. Could Seb have been right yet again? Was Nick indeed the man I needed right now?

He had to be. There was no one else.

'Do you want me to come and get you?' he said curtly, answering on the first ring.

I swallowed hard, hating the tightness of my throat and the crushing pressure on my chest, hat-

ing my despair and dependency, especially on him.
'If it's not too much trouble.'

'I'll be there in an hour.'

CHAPTER FOUR

THE CLOUDS HAD thickened quite a bit by the time we arrived back on Suza, Nick's island, but that was about as much of the journey as I registered. Stunned and distraught, I'd barely been aware of even moving as I'd packed up my things and settled my bill, let alone taken note of my surroundings or the man who'd so swiftly come to my rescue. I'd lost the capacity for speech. Thoughts had spun through my head like the whirring engine of the boat carrying me and my suitcase to relative safety. Even the jarring bounciness of the waves couldn't distract me from the chaos roiling around inside me.

How could it be happening all over again? Where would I find the strength and resilience to get through it? Could I even begin to hope that in this clickbait-y world today's headlines would be tomorrow's fish and chips wrapping?

Every cell of my body was on the brink of splintering, I realised as Nick showed me to an elegant guest suite and set my suitcase beside the enormous bed. Tears of frustration and helplessness had been stinging my eyes since I'd read the headlines and my nerves were stretched to snapping point. But I refused to break down in front of him. He'd run a mile, no doubt with a sigh of yet more exasperation at my drama, and then I'd have another thing to feel awkward about.

'I'll leave you to settle in,' he said, his jaw set, his expression stony, the irritation I could feel vibrating off him completely understandable when my being here had to be disruptive, inconvenient and the very last thing he needed.

I swallowed hard and accepted the guilt as just one more emotion piling in on top of the rest. 'I'm so sorry about all this.'

He shot me a dark, frustrated look. 'How is it your fault?'

'Isn't everything?'

'No.'

'It certainly feels as though it is,' I said, my voice thick, my throat tight. 'I'm the one who lived a shallow and frivolous life back then and was regularly photographed stumbling out of taxis before falling from grace. I'm the one with the winning lottery ticket now. But thank you for coming to my rescue. I had no one else to call.'

Something flickered in the depths of his eyes, but it had vanished before I could even begin to decipher it. 'Not a problem,' he said, turning on his heel and heading for the door. 'If you need anything, let me know.'

I felt marginally stronger after a weep fest and a shower, but I had no doubt it would take a lot more than that to unravel the tangle of emotions churning through me. On top of everything else that had happened recently, processing this latest development was simply too much for my poor battered and bruised brain to handle.

As if in solidarity, the puffiness of my eyes and the redness of my nose were proving an insurmountable challenge for my make-up, and as I stared at myself in the mirror, flinching at my reflection, I was sorely tempted to hole up in my room until I'd made sense of everything going on. Only when I'd constructed a rock-solid facade of cool indifference would I be ready to face my reluctant host.

But that could take days and I couldn't stand the idea of being alone with my tumultuous thoughts for a moment longer. They were too huge, too complicated, too overwhelming and I was teetering on the brink of total collapse. Nick had said to let him know if I needed anything, and right now I needed a distraction. I'd already texted Seb to let him know where I was, and reading the hundreds of emails that were still flooding in appealed about as much as morbidly scouring the headlines. But there was always the financial planning report Nick had sent. *That* required attention. So, having shoved on a pair of sunglasses to achieve the result that make-up had failed to do, I lifted my chin, pulled my shoulders back and headed downstairs.

Following the faint sounds of his voice, I found him in a room that had to be his study, facing the window and staring out to sea with his big broad back to me. He was raking one hand through his hair in what looked like a gesture of frustration and holding his phone to his ear with the other.

'I want them gone,' he was saying with a cutting coldness that sent a shiver down my spine despite the heavy warmth of the air breezing in through the window and fluttering the papers on the enormous mahogany desk. 'The pictures. The articles. The photographers. I don't care what it costs. Just get it done. Now.'

He hung up and turned slightly to stash the phone in the back pocket of his jeans and went still when he caught sight of me. He looked me up and down in a way that made me strangely aware of what I was wearing—a short yellow dress with spaghetti straps that suddenly felt a lot skimpier than when I'd put it on—and for the briefest, most bizarre of moments I forgot how to breathe. My lungs seized. My breasts tightened and tingled, and my temperature shot so high I felt as if I were about to spontaneously combust.

But before I could work out what on earth was going on, his dark, unexpectedly stormy gaze landed on my face and his brows snapped together, which instantly refocused my attention and loosened my chest enough for me to breathe and my brain enough to engage.

'Who was that?' I said, making a pre-emptive strike designed to deflect both a remark on the evidence of my earlier distress, and—an even greater threat to what little self-possession I was clinging onto—an albeit unlikely enquiry into how I might be feeling.

'My head of PR.'

'Were you discussing me and the situation I find myself in?'

'Yes.'

Of course he was. I wasn't surprised. Despite his earlier 'not a problem', I knew I was exactly that. 'I completely understand your wish to rectify things.'

'Do you?' he said with a slight rise of his eyebrows. 'I doubt it.'

'It's obvious. The sooner the furore dies down, the sooner I can go home and leave you in peace.'

Something undefinable flitted across his face. 'Peace would be good,' he muttered darkly. 'In fact, peace would be excellent.'

'Can you really make it all go away with a phone call?' I asked, ignoring the odd tightening of my chest at the confirmation that he *really* didn't want me here and wondering instead if he could possibly be that powerful.

'A couple of phone calls,' he corrected. 'And yes. I can.'

Right. Obviously he was that powerful. Which was strange when I could still remember him as the gawky guarded teenager who'd first come to stay. But he now had billions and money talked.

'I can't help wondering how the press got hold of the news in the first place,' I said, stepping into the room and catching up some papers that had blown off the desk and were fluttering to the floor. 'And who put two and two together and came up with the conclusion that former wild-child social-ite Amelia Huntington-Smith and plain old office manager Millie Smith were one and the same.'

'You sound as though you suspect me.'

What? I straightened abruptly and stared at him. 'That's absurd. You'd have zero to gain, and, de-spite the fact that we are very much not friends,

I really can't see you engaging in anything quite so underhand.'

'It's a relief to know you trust me,' he said dryly.

'I do with my money. And that's all that matters. But nevertheless, *someone* leaked it.'

'And I have *someone* looking into it.'

'Who?'

'An investigator I use to dig into the backgrounds of all potential clients before I take them on.'

'Did you dig into me?'

'No need.'

I bristled at the bold certainty of his tone. 'You don't know *everything* about me, Nick,' I said. In fact, he hardly knew anything. He just thought he did.

'I know you're not a money launderer.'

True, but conceding a point to him had never appealed and it didn't now, so instead I dialled back to the fact he'd put an investigator on the case. 'What will you do if you get a name?'

'*When* I get a name,' he said, 'I will ensure they never work again.'

'Wow,' I said, impressed despite myself. He'd do that for me? For my family? Surely he didn't owe us that much? Then again, he was my brother's best friend and true friends helped each other out. Or so I'd heard. 'Thank you. I think.'

'You're welcome.'

'What did Seb say when you spoke to him?' I asked, trying not to feel hurt that my brother hadn't rung me back before asking Nick to rescue me yet again.

A trace of bafflement flickered across his face. 'I haven't spoken to him for weeks.'

Oh. 'Then you're not acting on his behalf?'

'No.'

Right. On reflection, though, I didn't know why that came as a surprise. Nick had always had bags of initiative. He didn't sit around waiting for life to happen to him. How else would he have made so much money before hitting thirty? 'I imagine your innate sense of justice would override any iffy personal feelings you might bear a person.'

His eyebrows lifted. 'My innate sense of justice?'

'It's not as if you're acting out of any particular concern for my welfare, is it?'

'Why wouldn't I be?'

'Because you can't be any more concerned with my welfare than I am with yours.'

He looked a bit taken aback by that and I regretted being quite so honest, but it was nothing but the truth and I couldn't quite bring myself to apologise.

'Was there something you wanted, Amelia?'

I shook off the twinge of something that felt oddly like disappointment—ridiculous when I didn't even *want* him to be concerned about me or vice versa—and reminded myself of why I'd sought him out. 'I thought we might take this opportunity to go through your report.'

'Now?'

'If you're not busy with something else.'

His response, when it came, was lukewarm. 'I suppose it has to be done at some point.'

'Great.'

In response to Nick's muttered, 'Have a seat,' I sat down while he fiddled around on his computer. As the printer began spewing out pages, I thought about the icy tone with which he'd issued his instructions to his head of PR and the strangely fierce expression he'd adopted when he'd clearly noted I'd been upset.

For the briefest of moments he'd looked as if he'd wanted to rip things apart with his bare hands and I couldn't help wondering as I watched him gather up the sheets and staple them together what it would be like to have someone who offered that level of unwavering support on your side, who instinctively fought your corner. A person might be able to achieve anything they wanted with that kind of backing. They could try everything, secure in the knowledge they'd have the best of safety nets if it all went wrong, and figure out at leisure who they really were and where they fitted in the world.

Not that I'd ever experience anything like that. Until I overcame my trust, self-esteem and guilt issues—which were so deep-rooted they were now an integral part of me and therefore pretty damn insurmountable—it simply wouldn't happen. And that was fine. Self-reliance was *my* safety net. My only one, sure, but an excellent one nonetheless. So there was no point wishing things were different or envying those for whom relationships were easy. I just had to get on with things and focus on a future that would take up all my time and require all my energy anyway.

Nick handed me a copy of his report and then folded his large frame into the seat on his side of the desk. 'Have you read it?'

'Briefly.'

'Shall I summarise?'

'Please do.'

Flicking back and forth between the pages with one hand while spinning a pen around his fingers of his other, he started by reiterating my wishes and then moved on to his suggestions for facilitating them. From there, he segued into a complicated and detailed description of suitable investment options and products and the deployment of fiendishly clever fiscal vehicles and mechanisms, which

I followed for a while until my fascination with his mouth took over and zoned me out.

Mesmerised by the way it moved, I could hardly take my eyes off it. His lips came together, then parted to reveal the flash of white teeth and a tantalising glimpse of his tongue, and did it all on repeat. How had I never noticed its sensuality before? Because it generally took the form of a grim flat line whenever he turned in my direction? Or on occasion, curled into a faint twist of disapproval? And why did I suddenly long to know how it would feel—hard and passionate on mine or light and teasing as it travelled over my skin?

'Amelia.'

At the terse delivery of my name, I blinked and came to, snapping my gaze up to his and battling the violent blush I could feel sweeping right through me. 'Yes?'

'I asked if you had any questions.'

Questions? About what? I hadn't taken in a word. But he didn't need to know that. Nor, thank God, since I was still wearing my sunglasses, could he have any idea I'd been transfixed by his mouth.

Sternly reminding myself to focus on the reason I was sitting opposite him, I took a deep breath, banished the feverish heat from my body and pulled myself together. 'No,' I said with a brief nod and a cool smile. 'No questions. That all seems very comprehensive. Very thorough. I'd expect nothing less from the best. Although given your competence in this area, I am somewhat surprised you haven't yet found me an island.'

'It's been a week,' he said bluntly. 'I work fast, but not that fast.'

'My fake advisors found me one within three days.'

He arched one dark eyebrow. 'And you didn't find that unlikely?'

'Funnily enough, the private island real estate market isn't something I'm an expert on.'

'Which was why you were such an easy target.'

Ouch. 'Thank you for pointing that out.'

He sat back, rested his elbows on the arms of his chair, still rolling the pen around his long tanned fingers. 'On the subject of islands, though, it would be useful for planning purposes to know what you intend for yours.'

'I can email you the folder,' I said, determinedly keeping my eyes off his hands, off his mouth, off everything but his eyes and thinking instead of my research. My report was ten times the length of his. He wasn't the only thorough one. Mine had pictures. Maps. Links. Even a glossary, which, come to think of it, his could have done with.

'An outline will do.'

Would it? I wasn't so sure. I hadn't told anyone the full extent of my dreams. Not even Seb. They were so personal, so fragile. On the other hand, how could Nick help with the implementation of my plans if I didn't share the details with him? Might he have some advice? He did own an island himself, after all.

'Promise you won't laugh?'

'Why would I do that?'

'You may well think I'm overreaching and question my sanity. Even I swing between convincing myself it's the best idea on the planet to wondering what on earth I think I'm doing when I'm anything but an expert.'

'I promise I won't laugh.'

'All right,' I said, mentally crossing my fingers and hoping for the best, which was basically Nick listening and absorbing and not responding with disbelieving scorn. 'So, as I mentioned when I was here last, one of the areas I'm interested in exploring is the revival of coral reefs. Quite apart from being an important ecosystem for underwater life, they protect shorelines from the effects of hurricanes. They provide millions of people with a crucial source of income. Did you know that the tiny animals that build them offer the potential to develop new drugs to treat disease?'

'I did not.'

I scoured his expression for signs of disdain, but could see none, so judged it safe to continue. 'No, well, it's a little-known fact,' I said. 'Anyway, because of overfishing, pollution, oceanic acidification, not to mention general man-made destruction, the reefs could disappear within thirty years. But it doesn't have to be terminal. Marine protected areas—sort of giant national parks in the ocean—can help make reefs healthier and more resilient. And genetics are important too. One day, scientists might be able to develop coral that can cope with the marine conditions and restore the reefs.'

'Really?'

'Yes,' I said, warming to my theme. 'But mainly, though, my interest lies in the hawksbill turtle. I saw one once in the Great Barrier Reef and it was love at first sight. They're magnificent creatures. Their shells are exquisite. I've made a study of them. They help maintain the health of the reef. They use their pointy beaks to feed on the sponges that feed off the reef's surface. They've been around for the last hundred million years, but over the last century their population has declined by four fifths. There are only eight thousand left. This is not good, I think you'll agree, and I'd like to set up a breeding programme to increase their numbers. Ideally, I'd buy a landmass that came with a reef and the potential to achieve all this as well as recruit the necessary personnel. So there you have it. Those are my plans, in a nutshell.'

I stopped and waited for a response, but Nick didn't seem to be paying attention. He was staring at my mouth in much the same way I'd been staring at his earlier. His eyes were dark and a faint frown creased his brow. He couldn't possibly have been distracted by my impassioned speech as I had when he'd been talking about financial products, could he? No. The idea of it was absurd. Whatever he was doing, he was *not* entertaining thoughts of kissing me. I probably had something stuck in my teeth—yet another cause for disapproval, no doubt.

'Nick.'

He blinked and gave his head a quick shake. 'What?'

'Are you even listening?'

He shifted in his seat, as if trying to ease some kind of discomfort and, with a faint wince, pulled his seat forward and rested his elbows on the desk. 'Of course I'm listening,' he said, his voice a little gruff. 'Coral reefs and hawksbill turtles. Marine protection areas and breeding programmes. Quite a departure from stationery.'

'Stationery has never been my passion. It's hard to get excited about paper-clip orders and A3 supply issues. Tropical waters, and what lives in them, on the other hand, have been something of an obsession of mine ever since I learned how to dive with my father. I even studied marine biology once upon a time.'

'I remember.'

'The fact that I didn't get to finish my degree is something I'd like to rectify,' I said. 'If I can get back on a course, that is. It's been a long time. My studying skills are rusty and it's entirely possible I wouldn't be intellectually up to it. But I'm willing to give it a shot.'

'You'd be more than intellectually up to it.'

I sat back, momentarily stunned. 'Is that a compliment?'

'No. It's a fact,' he countered. 'And here's another. You didn't have to quit in the first place.'

In response to that, my eyebrows shot up and my jaw dropped. What on earth was he talking about? At the time, Nick had been off forging his own future but he'd known full well what was going on in the Huntington-Smith world. Thanks to the tabloids, everyone had.

'Of course I did,' I said flatly. 'I had no means of funding the course and a six-figure credit-card debt to pay off.'

'You could have accepted my money.'

'Well, yes, in theory I could have, I suppose,' I conceded, although back then, with my entire life crumbled to dust, I'd been in no fit state to do anything. 'But I would still have had to pay it back. You or the bank. It made no difference. I would have had to get a job to pay the bills either way.'

'You wouldn't have had to pay it back.'

I stared at him. 'What?'

'What I offered you wasn't a loan,' he said. 'It was a gift.'

A gift? I frowned. 'Are you sure?'

'I'm hardly likely to forget.'

No. I wasn't likely to forget that particular encounter either. It had not been pleasant. 'I didn't know that.'

'You didn't give me a chance to explain.'

That was true. I'd rejected it out of hand barely before he'd finished what he was saying. He'd unexpectedly turned up at my flat one evening shortly after my father's death, immaculate in a five-thousand-pound suit, not a hair out of place. Flustered, wretched, and acutely aware of how shabby I and my environs looked in comparison to him, I'd just wanted him gone. 'But why would you offer me a gift?'

'Because I could.'

'Any opportunity to rub my nose in our reversal of fortune, right?' I said a touch bitterly, remembering all too clearly how humiliated I'd felt, how much I'd hated him in that moment for reminding me how far I'd fallen and how much I'd lost.

A thundering silence followed my words. Nick visibly recoiled and paled beneath his tan, a tiny muscle pounding in his jaw. 'Is that what you think I was doing?'

'I don't blame you,' I said, the memories that were descending thick and fast accelerating my pulse and tightening my chest. 'I deserved it.'

'You didn't deserve any of it.'

I did. After all, I'd once rubbed his nose in the material differences between us, hadn't I? Furthermore, I'd destroyed my family, and, however unintentional, there was no absolution for that.

'And you could not be more wrong about my reason for offering you the money.'

'Then what *were* you doing?'

'You'd suffered enough.'

I stared at him, my stomach beginning to churn. 'So it was pity?'

'No.'

'Charity?'

'No.'

But it had to have been at least one of those two things because if it wasn't revenge what else was there? It had never occurred to me that Nick had felt sorry for me. The thought of it, the realisation that he might continue to do so, made me feel physically sick. Disapproval and disdain I could just about handle. Pity, with the hateful weakness and helplessness it invoked, I could not.

'Well, whether it was a gift or a loan,' I said, suddenly desperate to redress the balance, to try and claw back some modicum of dignity, 'I'm glad I didn't take your money. It's impossible to overstate how much I would have hated being beholden to you. I'm not all that thrilled about it now, to be honest. I loathe the fact that I need your help. I can't stand it that I had to ask you to come and pick me up from Zanzibar. I didn't want your charity or your pity or any special favours then, and I certainly don't want them now. And before you claim again that you weren't motivated by either, you tell me why a man driven solely by money would still not have sent me a contract or details of his fees.'

I stopped, my heart pounding and my head spinning, the silence thundering. Nick's expression revealed a split second of shock before it became utterly blank, and his voice, when he spoke, was cold and clipped. 'I'll get onto it right away.'

CHAPTER FIVE

BECAUSE I WAS desperate to flee the suddenly horribly tense atmosphere in the study and needed to sort through everything that was swirling around in my head with increasingly hammering persistence, I took a walk outside.

All Nick had said when I'd abruptly announced my intention to get some air and surged to my feet was a curt, 'Stick to the paths.' He could have been shocked, he could have been furious, he could have been relieved. The ice-cold impassivity that had descended over him made it impossible to tell.

I followed his undoubtedly prudent advice and set off down a wide sandy track that wound through vegetation that grew denser and lusher the further I progressed into it. The rustling palms and heavily laden fruit trees were alive with caws and squawks. Brightly coloured butterflies of all hues and sizes fluttered around bushes from which came chirrups and squeaks. I could feel and smell the heat and humidity as if they were tangible.

At the westernmost point of the island, as far from the villa as it was possible to get, I came across a second jetty, next to which was a boat-house that contained several surfboards, a kayak and sails of various shapes and sizes.

In one of the white sandy coves I wandered down to, I found, among the driftwood that had washed up on the shore, a metre-long coconut crab and two green sea turtles. I sat on a rock and spent a good ten minutes watching a fish eagle hovering twenty metres above the surface of the sea and then swooping down majestically to capture its prey.

But Nick's island wasn't quite the tropical paradise now it had seemed the day I'd originally turned up. Unlike then, this evening's sun kept disappearing behind ever billowing clouds. The air was growing increasingly thick and heavy and the swell of the sea seemed to be rising. There was a sense of turbulence and disruption rippling through my surroundings, and it matched exactly the uneasy churning of my thoughts.

When I recalled the way in which the conversation Nick and I had had earlier had ended, I was swamped with remorse and mortification. I didn't think I'd ever forget the glimpse of stark shock I'd caught before he'd retreated behind a wall of stone. For a split second, he'd looked as if I'd struck him, somehow wounded, but then why wouldn't he? For all his imperviousness towards me, he had to have *some* sort of feelings and my words had been harsh.

That I'd been thrown off balance by shameful memories and the discovery that he'd pitied me was no excuse. Once again backed into a corner and on the attack, I'd let my emotions get the better of me and lashed out. I'd laid waste to the veneer of civility we'd always maintained and been unpardonably rude, while he—with the exception of the odd pointed comment or two—had been nothing but supportive. He hadn't had to agree to help me with my fortune. He hadn't had to rescue me from Zanzibar. And yet I'd told him I resented it all.

What on earth had I been thinking? I wondered as I took a breather and stood on a promontory from which I could see for miles. Had I completely lost my mind? Until a contract was signed, Nick could withdraw from the deal at any moment, leaving me in as vulnerable and exposed a position as before. What if he sent me packing and to hell with the press attention back home? I'd only have myself to blame. But more importantly, I wasn't that person any more. I wasn't reckless and rash and I didn't speak without thinking.

Burning up with shame and the need to put things right—and not just because I did, in fact, need his help—I returned to the villa with far less regard for the scenery than I'd had when I set out.

By following the mouth-watering scents of ginger and garlic, I found Nick this time in the kitchen. He was standing at the hob that was embedded in the island, agitating a frying pan. His hair was wet and he'd changed clothes, which suggested he'd taken a shower, but judging by the tension radiating off him and the rigidity of his jaw it hadn't been a relaxing one.

Bracing myself for a hostile reception—inevitable, given the chill with which he'd sent me off on my walk, and totally deserved given my inability to get a grip on my emotional volatility—I took a deep breath and tried not to think about the unpleasant way my dress was sticking to my skin.

'Something smells good,' I said, nerves nevertheless tangling in my stomach as I advanced towards him.

He glanced up at me, his eyes shuttered, his expression unfathomable. 'How was your walk?'

'Breezy.'

'You were gone a long time.'

'It's a beautiful island.'

'It is.'

'I came across a boathouse.'

'Did you?'

'Are all the boards and boats and other things in it yours?'

'Yes.'

'Do you use them?'

'When I'm not working.'

All too easily I could see him kayaking around the island and kite-surfing across the sea—no wonder he had muscles and a tan—and it was with quite some effort that I hauled my thoughts into line. I was on a mission and I would not be derailed.

'I'm sorry for what I said earlier,' I said, hopping onto a stool and battling back a fresh wave of remorse at the memory of it. 'All those things about charity and favours and about hating the fact that you're having to help me. I haven't had to rely on anyone for eight years and it's taking some getting used to. And then there's the stress I've been under lately, what with everything that's been going on. Nevertheless, none of that is any excuse. I overreacted. I was rude. I apologise.'

Not a muscle flickered in response to my words, which was disappointing but not entirely unexpected when he'd never made it easy for me to apologise. 'I've emailed you a contract,' he said, abandoning the pan and wiping his hands with a cloth. 'And details of my fees.'

'Thank you. I'll take a look later.'

'Drink?' He tossed the cloth into the sink then nodded in the direction of the tall glass in front of me that looked to be a gin and tonic, judging by the cubes of ice and the sprig of rosemary.

'You must have read my mind.' I half expected a flash of alarm to skitter across his face, but he remained as taciturn as ever. 'However, I'm glad you can't,' I added, reaching for the glass as if it were a lifeline. 'My mind is a mess.' I took a fortifying sip of my drink and sighed in appreciation as the fragrant scent of rosemary wafted into my head and the alcohol hit my blood. 'This, on the other hand,' I said, putting the glass back down, 'is perfect. My favourite combination.'

'I'm not solely driven by money, Amelia.'

In surprise, I jerked my gaze to his and found him looking at me with an intriguing intensity. Had I hit a nerve? Was that a hint of vulnerability I could hear? How interesting. 'It would be understandable if you were.'

'Because of where I come from?'

'It's nothing to be ashamed of.'

'I'm not. The circumstances in which I grew up were wholly beyond my control. Shame stems from things that have been done badly and could have been done differently. Things over which you *do* have control.'

Yes, well, I knew all about that, and I had the feeling that he knew I knew. 'Believe me,' I said, shifting on the stool to ease my sudden discomfort, 'if I could go back and do my time again, there are many things I'd do differently.'

'Like what?'

'How long do you have?'

'However long it takes.'

If that were true, he'd be waiting a long time because it was never going to happen. Apologising for my bad manners was one thing, baring my soul to a man who had such a low opinion of me was quite another. And why was he so interested in my shortcomings anyway? So he could gather together yet more ammunition to use against me?

'I'll bear that in mind,' I said, having no intention of giving him a reason to think even less of me than he already did. 'So what else *does* drive you, apart from money?'

'Prudent planning. Tax efficiency. Taking the best care I can of the assets my clients have and solving their problems.'

Such as mine? 'Talking of problematic clients,' I said, sternly reminding myself that the only assets I wanted him taking care of were financial ones, 'is there any news on the press frenzy back home?'

'Not yet.'

Oh, dear. That didn't bode well. How long was

it going to be until the fuss had died down back home and it was safe for me to leave? How much more of this awkwardness, this stalking each other like caged tigers, were we going to have to tolerate?

Maybe time would pass more quickly with conversation. Maybe I could implement the strategy I'd developed on the plane over to rise above such small-mindedness with maturity and serenity by doubling down on the small talk. It was worth a try.

'What's for supper?'

'Red snapper.'

'Delicious,' I said, my stomach giving a faint rumble. 'My diet over the last eight or so years has consisted mainly of soup and pasta. This last week I've been making up for lost time by ordering seafood whenever I can, and it's been heavenly. How can I help?'

'You can lay the table,' he said, selecting a long knife from a rack and beginning to sharpen it on a steel with the expertise of a professional chef not unlike the one who'd come to teach me and ten of my friends how to prepare sushi for my twelfth birthday. 'Plates and cutlery are in the cupboard in front of you. There's a salad in the fridge.'

I busied myself with setting the table, pleased to have something to focus on other than all that efficient competence, which was oddly mesmerising and unaccountably compelling, as well as the memories of the once golden, now tainted times I'd had as a child. 'I didn't realise you cooked.'

'How else am I going to feed myself?'

'I don't know,' I said, straightening a fork. I'd never given it any thought. Why would I? I'd only mentioned it to fill the prickly silence. 'Order in?'

'Where from?'

It had been a joke—not one of my best, admittedly—but as I glanced out into the dark starless night, it occurred to me that Nick made an unsettling point. We weren't in London, where food delivery was one click of an app away. We were out here on a small island off the east coast of Africa, surrounded by the Indian Ocean, all alone, just the two of us. Rustling up a simple supper in a low-lit kitchen to the sounds of a seething sea and the warm humid breeze swishing through the leaves of his palm trees outside.

Which, come to think of it, felt unexpectedly intimate, I reflected uneasily as I headed to the fridge. We'd never been alone together before. At least, not like this. There'd been that one time when he'd picked me up from a party in London I hadn't been finding all that much fun and driven me home in stony silence, but that had been different. I'd been seventeen and on a mission to get over my crush on him. He'd been nineteen and with one of his interchangeable leggy blondes, who he'd ousted from the passenger side of his second-hand two-seater convertible with a smouldering smile filled with sensual promise that had filled me with envy.

But while I'd been so achingly aware of him sitting close beside me, and I could still recall every moment of it all these years later, my skin hadn't prickled on that occasion as it was suddenly prickling now. I hadn't experienced then quite the fire that was currently rushing along my veins. There'd been far less of a buzz, far fewer butterflies, and any burning up inside had been down to helpless, sullen jealousy.

'So where do you get supplies?' I asked, determinedly focusing on the pedestrian and reminding myself that not only was it stiflingly warm this evening—hence the fire and the prickling, obviously—but also that Nick and I were anything but intimate. We were tolerating each other's company under duress. There was nothing romantic about any of this, and why was I even *thinking* of romance?

'I have a delivery from the mainland once a week,' he said, sliding the snapper from the pan onto a board and proceeding to de-bone it with the newly sharpened knife. 'And I fish.'

I set the salad on the table and stared at him, unable to contain my amazement. 'You fish?'

He paused mid slice and glanced up at me. 'Why the surprise?'

'I don't know,' I said, flustered by the sardonic tinge to his words and the lingering concerns about intimacy. 'I guess it just doesn't fit with the image I've always had of you. The sharp suit… The pristine shirt… The polished shoes…'

'I'm not always in a suit.'

No. He wasn't. This evening he was wearing faded jeans and a pink—pink!—shirt that was, of all astonishing things, untucked. He might have had a shower, but he hadn't shaved, and a faint five o'clock shadow adorned his jaw. With his thick dark hair touching his collar instead of being closely cropped as usual he looked…untamed. Almost piratical. Which, I had to admit, was an exceptionally good look on him.

I could hardly believe that I'd met him eighteen years ago and had thought I had him all worked out. Clearly I knew nothing. Not that I needed to know anything, of course. He was my financial advisor, that was it. Whether his rigidly controlled guard ever came down was no more my business than what might lie behind it. Which version of himself he preferred—immaculately suited or casually beachified—was of no interest to me whatsoever. Continuing the conversation, however, to keep my mind from frustratingly wandering down inappropriate avenues, *was* important, even if it did feel like wading through treacle.

'Did you catch this?' I asked as he placed a fillet on each plate and brought them to the glass-topped driftwood dining table that easily sat twelve.

'Yes. This morning.'

An unnecessary and unwelcome vision of him at the helm of a brilliant white yacht, shirtless, muscles flexing as he threw out a line, shot into my head before I despairingly shoved it right out again.

'I'm impressed,' I said, sitting down and flapping out a napkin.

'So easily?'

Why I'd imagined him semi-naked might be incomprehensible but at least I could understand his icy scepticism. Once upon a time, in my circle of so-called friends, disdain, feigned or genuine, had been cool, which was obviously anything but cool. 'People change.'

'Do they?' He took the seat opposite me and seemed to fill my vision despite the width of the table.

'Well, some do,' I said, inordinately grateful for the intricate wooden structure that supported the glass slab and would prevent any accidental bumping of knees. 'You haven't. You're more consistent than anyone else I know.'

'In what way?'

Ah. So that had been a silly thing to say because now I had to come up with examples. And since I had no intention of embarking on a lengthy explanation of exactly how I knew what his opinion of me had been for the last decade or so—which might suggest I cared when I absolutely didn't—I had to rack my brains for something more prosaic.

'Well, obviously the evidence is limited,' I said, faintly surprised to discover that I didn't have to rack them for long. 'But whenever I see you, you always have the top two buttons of your shirt undone. You have a habit of spinning things around your fingers. Toothpick, beer mat, coin, pen. Whatever's to hand. You walk into the bar, the room, or wherever it is we happen to find ourselves unavoidably in the same vicinity and you look first right, then left and then you frown, as if you're searching for something or someone and you're annoyed you can't find them. You're perpetually displeased to see me and your girlfriends are, without fail, tall and blonde and never last longer than a month.'

At that, a flicker of alarm did dart across his face. 'I had no idea you were so perceptive.'

Neither did I, come to think of it.

'There are lots of things you don't know about me,' I said coolly, picking up my knife and fork and assuring myself that the flutter of my stomach was down to hunger, not unease. 'The main one being that, unlike you, I *have* changed.'

'Have you?'

'I had no choice. I was appalling.'

'You were spoilt.'

'I was,' I agreed. 'I was an obnoxious brat. As you once so eloquently pointed out. At my six-teenth birthday party, if I recall correctly.'

'You wanted me to be your plaything.'

Another moment I wasn't particularly proud of, I thought with a wince that I didn't even try to hide. Midway through an afternoon of hanging out by the pool, egged on by my so-called friends at the time, I'd sauntered up to him and demanded he come and entertain us. When he'd icily refused, I'd muttered something about chips and shoulders, told him he wasn't good enough for us anyway and sashayed away.

In my defence—not that I deserved one—I'd been all shaken up inside. Nick had been the topic of conversation and it had confused the hell out of me. Up until then he'd barely been on my radar. He'd simply been a friend of Seb's, who, since his mother lived four hundred miles north of the school and worked all hours, and his father wasn't in the picture, often came to stay at weekends and during the holidays, but ultimately had been as unworthy of interest as my brother.

However, that afternoon, I'd seen him for the first time through my friends' eyes—an eighteen-year-old hunk with a tall athletic frame and a brooding way about him that had suddenly sent shivers down my spine and my hormones into overdrive. In response to the chaos caused by the buzz of attraction that had weakened my limbs and accelerated my pulse and the sting of his rejection that had hurt more than I could possibly have imagined, I'd behaved cruelly and clumsily and I could absolutely understand why from that day forward he'd treated me with such contempt.

'I didn't really,' I muttered, feeling my cheeks turning beetroot as I cut off a bite-sized chunk of fish. 'I was impressionable and had lousy friends. They bet me to get you to hang out with us. I should have said no and left you alone. I should never have insulted you the way I did. I'm so sorry. It was unforgivable. I didn't even mean it. I realise the apology comes thirteen years too late, but you have it nonetheless.'

For a moment he just looked at me, his eyes dark and locked onto mine, while my heart thumped so loudly I could hear it in my ears. Then he said,

'I neither want or need it,' and it was like a slap across the face.

My breath caught. My flush deepened. No. Well. That was fair enough. I'd always known I'd burned virtually every one of the few bridges we'd shared. It had never bothered me before. Somehow, it did now. My throat was tight with shame. Regret was stabbing me in the chest. And for the life of me I couldn't work out why. It wasn't as if I wanted to play with him now. 'I understand.'

'You couldn't even *begin* to understand,' he said with equal bluntness, but this time I didn't flinch. I didn't react at all. Because it was becoming pretty bloody clear I understood absolutely nothing.

The end of the meal couldn't come fast enough. Despite my best efforts to keep up the small talk, conversation became increasingly stilted. My barrel-scraping questions and observations about island wildlife, water sports and the welfare of his mother met with ever more monosyllabic responses and an ever-deepening frown.

'What's the one thing you want but you don't have?' I asked, doggedly determined to keep going in an effort to avoid long, uncomfortable silences.

'Peace and quiet.'

'Where do you see yourself in five years' time?'

'Working. Making more money to give away.'

'Give away?'

'I fund bursaries. Scholarships. Charities that support those kids that want to do better but are held back by where they've come from.'

That was admirable. But then presumably there were only so many penthouses and islands one man could buy. 'What are you afraid of?'

'That your questions will never come to an end.'

They did after that. I was all out of small talk. Which was a shame because without that to focus on, to my intense frustration, I found it almost impossible not to keep staring at him. He was so big, so close, and right in my line of vision. My gaze kept snagging on his hands and his mouth as he sliced up the fish and ate. Bizarrely, a vision of him surging to his feet, pulling me into his arms and spreading me across the table to do with me what he wanted took shape in my mind, and, once there, wouldn't shift.

My inability to keep a clear head around him was becoming increasingly intolerable. I loathed the way my self-control seemed to disappear in his vicinity and the jitters that took up residence inside me like a swarm of bees. I hated the fact that no matter how often I instructed myself to think of him in a purely professional context, I couldn't.

The second I got to my room I'd be calling James and arranging to be picked up just as soon as was humanly possible, I vowed as I put my knife and fork down and polished off what was left of my drink. Who cared about a raking-up of the past and a few crappy headlines? I was older and stronger this time around and I would *not* be a victim. Emails could easily be deleted. Spurious requests to connect on social media could easily be ignored. Of course I'd be able to recognise an ulterior motive. And after I'd explained, my colleagues would surely understand why I'd told them nothing of my win.

Once home, I need never speak to Nick again. We could communicate by email and revert to nods and a very wide berth on the unfortunate occasion our paths did have to cross in the future. Upon reflection, the status quo wasn't *that* bad.

'Right, well, thank you for supper,' I said, once the kitchen was clear of the most excruciating meal I'd had in years. 'And despite what I said earlier in your study, thank you for all your help too. I realise it didn't sound like it at the time, but I *am* grateful. I know how I'm lucky to have you. I mean your services, obviously,' I hastened to clarify, but it didn't sound much better, so I added, 'Or rather, your financial services,' which, to my despair, only made it worse.

Nick merely stood watching as I flushed and floundered and dug myself into an ever bigger hole and I felt like banging my head against the wall in frustration. Would I *ever* be able to speak to this man without my words producing an unintended consequence? Or was I a completely lost cause?

'Anyway, you'll no doubt be delighted to hear that I'll be out of your hair tomorrow,' I said, prepared to move heaven and earth to facilitate such a move if I had to. 'I'm aiming to be on a plane first thing.'

'That's not going to happen.'

My heart skipped a beat. What? No. Why? 'Do you have doubts about your influence over the press back home?'

'Not at all,' he said, with an ominous glance in the direction of the open French doors and the night beyond. 'I do, however, have doubts about the weather.'

CHAPTER SIX

IT WAS WITH a mixture of consternation and relief that I made my escape and fled to my room. But while the consternation over the weather and the implications of its deterioration lingered, the relief didn't last nearly as long.

I barely noticed the luxurious comfort of the space I occupied. I didn't have the wherewithal to appreciate the cool white walls, the honey-coloured wood floor and the soothingly neutral soft furnishings and I gave the gleaming en-suite only the most cursory of glances as I set the water temperature to cold and stepped into the enormous walk-in shower. I was too preoccupied with ruminating on the conversation Nick and I had had at supper, trying to unravel the myriad thoughts and questions swirling around my head and keeping my roiling emotions in check.

Why could I not stop thinking about him in inappropriate contexts? was the question uppermost in my mind as I brushed my teeth and climbed into bed. Such as a state of nakedness. Or a steamy embrace in which we kissed as if the world were about to end. Was the stress I'd been under finally taking its toll and breaking me down? Was it the shock of seeing him out of his usual environment? Spending time with him alone? What?

Surely I couldn't be attracted to him, I thought with a shiver of apprehension, lying there in the thick, heavy dark, a hot and achy pulse throbbing in the pit of my stomach. The crush I'd perversely developed on him in the aftermath of the pool party hadn't been *that* bad, even if once his many physical attributes had been pointed out, it had been annoyingly impossible to ignore them.

Although it had taken three years of determined effort—burning the candle at both ends by studying for my school exams during the term and partying hard in the holidays and my year off—I'd eventually got him out of my system. There was zero point in continuing to want him, I'd realised, gazing longingly at him one evening while subtly shooting daggers at the back of the girl he was with. He was never going to suddenly turn round and want me back. He went for tall willowy blondes, and, even without the complication of how little he thought of me, I was an average height curvy brunette.

I'd come to the decision that it was time to grow up and move on, and I genuinely assumed I had. I'd hung up my dancing shoes and accepted a university place in Zurich. I'd put my embarrassing youth behind me and knuckled down to study, my dream of working in marine conservation driving me to achieve top marks and become the best, until my family lost everything and my life imploded and I had to scrabble around in the rubble for some kind of future.

But what if I *hadn't* moved on? What if I'd merely buried the attraction beneath the weight of my studies and then the brutal upheaval of my existence, aided and abetted by Nick's continued disapproval of me? Could it have lain inside me all these years, dormant, like a volcano waiting to erupt?

No, I decided firmly as I tossed and turned, trying to find a cool spot in the bed. There was no volcano, dormant or otherwise. The fundamentals hadn't changed. He still dated blondes and he still loathed me. I'd be on a hiding to nothing, and I wasn't that much of an idiot.

My crazy response to him a week ago had to have been a result of the stress of the situation I'd found myself in messing with my reason. And now, most likely, it was the weather. No doubt the electricity that sizzled through me was down to the dark gathering clouds. The plummeting air pressure had to be responsible for the churning of my stomach, and it was the soaring heat and humidity of the air that had caused my core temperature to rise. It simply couldn't be anything else.

Nevertheless, despite these assurances, despite the thousand-thread-count sheets and the rhythmic rush of the sea, sleep was a long time coming.

I woke at six in the morning to an almighty clap of thunder and winds that sounded as though they were battering the palm trees and whipping up the sea. The hot air was suffocatingly thick and, within seconds, the faint patter of rain peppering the roof had turned into a deluge so loud I could barely hear myself think.

I groggily sat up and tried the switch of the bedside lamp to no avail, and my stomach plummeted. Nick had been right—I wasn't going anywhere today. Heaven and earth were indeed moving but instead of facilitating my escape, they were prohibiting it.

I got up to close the window I'd left open last night to alleviate the stifling heat and made my way across the dim, shadowy room, every muscle I possessed aching in protest. After such a fitful night, my eyes were gritty and sore. I felt as though I'd aged a hundred years and then been run over by a truck.

Everything was chaos, both inside and out, but there was no need to panic, I assured myself, breathing deeply and steadily as I stared out at the oppressive gunmetal sky through which not a single speck of blue peeked and the grey malevolently churning sea. I might have been on the back foot ever since the moment I'd contacted Nick requesting an appointment, but that didn't mean I had to remain there. All I had to do was locate my gumption and remind myself of my resolve to stay cool, collected and professional.

To that end, I would stop thinking about him naked. I would not entertain any more images of us kissing. I would get through the next day or two or however long the storm lasted by resolutely rising above such trivialities. By occupying the higher ground, as it were.

Of course there was no *literal* higher ground in the immediate vicinity but the house seemed sturdily built. Despite the gale that was howling outside, the window I'd just closed wasn't even rattling. I had nothing to worry about. Really. The tops of the palm trees might be being blown every which way but it wasn't as if debris were flying around. Presumably, Nick would have storm-proofed the house. A financial-planning guru would mitigate the risks and protect his assets, wouldn't he?

A sudden thump on my door made me jump back and shriek, and I had an instant vision of the roof nevertheless ripping off and all the furniture on the landing being swept up into the maelstrom.

'Amelia?'

Phew.

Not the roof.

Nick. My reluctant host, my sternest critic and very definitely not a man I was foolish enough to still be attracted to.

In an effort to calm my thundering pulse and quell my anxiety over both the weather and the havoc he played on my equilibrium, I pulled my shoulders back and set my jaw, then padded across the floor and opened the door. Storm lantern in hand, he stood on the landing looking dark and severe, tousled and stubbled and rumpled in a way that would have made me wonder if he'd just rolled out of bed had I been remotely interested in thinking of him along those lines, which I absolutely wasn't.

'Yes?'

'Put some clothes on and come downstairs,' he said tersely, having briefly raked his gaze over the white camisole and shorts set I was wearing, which was climate suitable but unfortunately left little to the imagination. 'Be quick. Take this.' He handed me a heavy torch from which shone a bright sweeping beam. 'And stay away from the windows.'

Five minutes later, I was sitting at one end of the cosy sofa that stood in the windowless inner hall of Nick's palatial villa, dressed in leggings and a sweatshirt, a combination that I trusted would meet with more approval than my nightwear. Under any other circumstances I might have bristled at the high-handed way he'd bossed me about, but under these, I had to admit I was rather glad he seemed to know what he was doing.

In addition to the lamp he'd been carrying earlier, a further three illuminated the space, two on the floor and one on each side table. Half a dozen torches were lined up on the console table that stood against the opposite wall, along with several bottles of water and a selection of snacks.

'So what exactly is this weather system we're currently experiencing?' I asked, eyeing the preparations warily, Nick's competence in this area not doing quite enough to completely erase my apprehension about the storm raging outside. 'A hurricane?'

He checked his phone, frowned, then tossed it aside and began to pace. 'A hurricane is known as a cyclone in these parts,' he muttered, clearly as frustrated as I was by the annoying turn of events that had screwed up both our plans. 'But no. It's a tropical depression.'

'What does that mean?'

'Light unorganised winds and minimal damage.'

There was a sudden crackle of lightning and a booming rumble of thunder that rent the air, both loud enough to make me want to cover my ears, and I didn't dare think about what stronger winds and less than minimal damage might mean.

'Is it likely to get worse?' I said, once the echoes had stopped reverberating off the walls and the flash of illumination had faded.

'Not according to the forecast,' he said. 'But that may change. Not that we'll know about it. The satellite dish is down and the electricity's cut out. For some reason the back-up generator hasn't kicked in.'

My stomach sank. Oh, dear. None of that sounded good. 'Can you fix it?'

'Probably. But voluntarily venturing outside right now would be lunacy. I secured the outdoor furniture last night just in case, but there's always the risk of a loose roof tile or the strike of an unexpectedly large wave.'

A vision of him lying bleeding on the terrace

and then being swept out to sea slammed into my head, and my heart gave a great lurch. My head swam and my stomach turned and for a moment I thought I might actually throw up.

'Could the island flood?' I asked, swallowing down the panic and assuring myself that since Nick, by his own admission, wasn't the reckless sort, that scenario was highly unlikely.

'It hasn't before.'

Before? 'How often does a storm like this hit?'

'Only once in the five years since I had the house built. That time it blew in the windows, but it was stronger.'

Hence his brusque instruction to steer clear of them. 'The hotel made no mention of anything.'

'It developed without warning,' he said. 'It happens.'

Much like his recent effect on me, I thought darkly, watching him shove his hands through his hair as he continued to glare at the floor and pace, about as removed from cool, in control and immaculate as it was possible to be. It had been years since he'd aroused anything other than frustrated irritation in me, yet from the moment I'd stepped foot on this island, I'd experienced virtually every emotion there was.

'How long do they last?' I asked, deciding it would be wise to focus on the practicalities instead of my intensely confusing and unwelcome response to him.

'If we're lucky, it'll be over in a matter of hours. If we aren't, it could be days.'

Days?

God.

'So what do we do in the meantime?'

He paused mid-step and shot me a look that was as dark and stormy as the sky. Something in it ignited a fire in the pit of my stomach and sent heat streaking along my veins. 'Sit it out.'

Sit it out? That wasn't what he'd been thinking. If it was, my heart wouldn't suddenly be thumping like a steam train and my mouth wouldn't be bone dry. But if it wasn't, then what *had* he been thinking? Why the flames? Why the burn? I had no idea. But did it matter? No. It did not.

What was important was remaining calm and in control. All I had to do was adapt to the situation. I was good at that. I'd had plenty of experience. Giving up a top university place to get a nine-to-five job. Swapping the beautiful Chelsea mansion for the grotty flat share in Hanwell. Getting round by sketchy public transport instead of a shiny chauffeur-driven Rolls. Budgeting, bargaining and the marked-down aisle at the supermarket. Vouchers, energy deals and a knackering weekend job in a bar. I'd got used to it all in the end.

So however long we were trapped here it would be fine. As I'd told myself repeatedly over the years, it was simply a question of mind over matter. The lanterns with their softly flickering light weren't romantic. They symbolised a potential catastrophic natural disaster. The confined space we occupied wasn't cosy. It was claustrophobic. Especially with Nick taking up so much room and stirring up the air with his incessant pacing. The tension radiating off him was making me feel as if I were sitting on knives. My nerves were buzzing and every time my supposedly loose top brushed against my body, shivers ran up and down my spine.

'Look, why don't you come and sit down?' I said, pushing up my sleeves and shifting to alleviate the prickling sensation, but only succeeding in tightening the fabric around my chest and making matters worse.

'I'm fine where I am,' he muttered, his gaze briefly flickering in my direction.

'You're making me nervous with all the pacing and glowering.'

'Too bad.'

'Did you not sleep well or something?'

'No,' he said, coming to an abrupt halt at the console table and grabbing a bottle of water. 'I did not sleep well.'

'Neither did I,' I replied. 'The heat was unbearable. I feel rough as anything.'

'It wasn't the heat,' he said, cracking open the lid and throwing me a pointed look that had me bristling.

'Are you saying it was me who kept you up?'

His expression darkened and something flared in the depths of his eyes that sent a hot shiver down my spine. 'That's exactly what I'm saying.'

His words were brusque, his voice was tight, and inwardly, I reeled. He didn't pull his punches. I knew my presence was a problem for him but, perhaps naïvely given last night's grumpiness, I hadn't expected quite this level of hostility. 'I'll be off as soon as I can.'

'It won't be soon enough.'

Well, to hell with chilly politeness. The gloves were now off. 'I realise the situation isn't ideal,' I said tartly, 'but—'

'Not ideal?' he cut in, the incredulity in his tone slicing through me like a knife. 'This situation is about as far from ideal as it's possible to get.'

Surely it wasn't *that* bad. We were safe. For now. Assuming the weather didn't worsen. 'Aren't you being a little overdramatic?'

'You're Seb's sister.'

I blinked in surprise at this non sequitur. 'What does that have to do with anything?'

'Apparently, not nearly enough.'

'No. Well. I can understand your concern. Naturally, you wouldn't want anything to happen to me on your watch. I mean, what would you tell Seb? But ultimately, I'm no one's responsibility but my own. And you didn't *have* to come and fetch me from Zanzibar, you know.'

He frowned. 'What?'

'You could have left me at the hotel.'

For a moment he just stared at me as if I'd grown two heads. Then he said, 'Could I?'

'Yes,' I said with a firm nod, not liking his condescending, knowing tone one little bit. 'I'd have been fine.'

'You called me wanting my help. You sounded far from fine. You sounded distraught. Do you seriously think I'd have ignored that?'

No, I had to acknowledge grudgingly, noting the tight set of his jaw and the resolve in his expression before he lifted the bottle to his mouth and poured half the contents down his throat. He wouldn't. Because, despite his many flaws, not all of his traits were unfortunate. Annoyingly, he had a decent streak a mile wide. He'd paid his mother back a hundred times over for her determination to see him succeed and the sacrifices she'd made to achieve that. He'd helped my brother out of a tight spot with his start-up and funded my mother's counselling course.

The instance he'd picked me up from that party wasn't the only time he'd fished me out of trouble. Once, when I was twelve, he'd sent packing the bunch of girls cornering me in the school dining room for reasons long since forgotten. On another occasion, he'd bodily removed a guy who'd been getting a little too handsy at the club in which we'd celebrated Seb's twenty-first birthday.

'OK, fine, you're right,' I said exasperatedly. 'I was distraught and I didn't give you a choice. But you were wrong about one thing.'

His brows snapped together. 'What?'

'This,' I said, waving a hand first at myself, next at his scowl and finally around the space, 'clearly *is* all my fault.'

He rolled his eyes.

He actually rolled his eyes.

And quite suddenly I'd had enough. Of his disapproval and his arrogance. Of the constant scepticism and the capacity he had to make me wither and squirm. Of my inability to simply brush it all off. It had been going on for years and I was sick of it.

With an urgency that came out of the blue to hit me square in the gut, I needed to know exactly what Nick thought of me and why. I wanted him to explain, so I could fix it. Because deep down I loathed the tension and the animosity that existed between us. The skirmishes that characterised our simmering battle of attrition were more wounding than I'd allowed myself to acknowledge. I couldn't stand seeing him when my brother was over from the States, or running into him as I occasionally did, and tensing right up, on edge and confused, unable to fully understand what was really behind the rock-bottom opinion he had of me.

Why did he refuse to see that I'd changed? I didn't make it *that* easy for him. I wasn't *always* deliberately flippant and silly. And why wouldn't he let me apologise for the mistakes I'd made over the years? Why wouldn't he grant me the forgiveness I badly wanted?

Despite my intention to simply rise above it all, I couldn't. If I was being brutally honest, frustrated irritation hadn't been the only emotion he'd roused in me over the last ten years or so. His attitude hurt. A lot. Here, now, was the opportunity to rectify any misapprehensions and get some answers. As soon as the weather improved I'd be off, and that would be that. Unaddressed, things between us would go back to the way they'd been before. And although I couldn't work out why, I truly didn't think I could bear it any more.

'What exactly is your problem with me, Nick?'

He went very still, the slight narrowing of his eyes his only movement. 'What on earth are you talking about? I have no problem with you.'

'Come off it,' I said, years of bottling it up unbottling as I leapt to my feet and took a step towards him. 'Every time our paths cross you can't help but look at me with disapproval. You practically quiver with it. You're dismissive and disdainful. I've been subjected to your stony glare and rigid jaw ever since that afternoon by the pool. Over a decade ago. And I get it. I was horrible back then. Selfish and arrogant and pampered. And I know I didn't behave any better when you offered me that loan, gift, whatever, five years later,' I continued hotly, on a roll now. 'But in mitigation, I was a wreck. My entire life had turned upside down. I'd just lost my home, my university place, my family, my sense of self, such as it was. I wasn't thinking straight. I was hurting. Humiliated. I didn't know what was what. My father had just died. My mother was no help and my brother was in the States. I didn't know where to turn. My boyfriend had dumped me and all my friends had vanished practically overnight.'

'*I* didn't.'

'*You* weren't a friend.'

His jaw tightened and his frown deepened. 'So you keep saying.'

'You never give me a chance to apologise for the things I've said or the way I've said them,' I said, ignoring the strange twist of my chest at whatever it was that flitted across his expression. 'Or explain. Every time I try, you just walk away or brush it off. You've been aloof and distant for years, and I want to know why. I'm not the person I used to be. I've learned to be better. Nicer. And I am. So why do you still hate me so much?'

'I don't hate you,' he said, a muscle hammering in his jaw and a dark flush tingeing his cheekbones. 'And I don't disapprove of you. I don't disapprove of you at all.'

I gave him a *yeah, right* look, but wasn't about to get into a 'yes, you did, no, I didn't' kind of a back and forth. 'Well, you make a damn good show of it,' I said, the evidence piling up in my head demanding a voice. 'Every time we meet and I try and say hello, you blank me. Whenever I say something— anything—you get this bored look on your face. You came to my rescue yesterday, yes, but it was clearly under duress, and at supper, you dismissed yet another attempt on my part to apologise for the things I've said and done. What else am I supposed to think other than that you loathe me?'

'That's never been my intention.'

'Then what *was* your intention?'

'Why do you care?'

That stopped me in my tracks, both literally and figuratively. I froze a foot away from him, my breath catching in my throat and my head spinning.

I didn't care.

Or did I?

If I didn't, his attitude towards me wouldn't have the power to hurt me. His rejection of my frequent attempts to apologise wouldn't have stung so badly. I wouldn't have felt the need to apologise in the first place. If I did, it would explain why I inevitably went home after encountering him feeling bruised and bewildered. Why the digs and the slights and the judgements had stuck to me like burrs.

I *did* care, I realised, feeling weak and a little light-headed. I wanted him to think better of me. I hated that he was still so wrong about me. As for the *why*, though, I hadn't a clue. 'I have no idea.'

'Well, when you find out, let me know,' he said. 'In the meantime, I think I *will* go and check on the generator, after all.'

CHAPTER SEVEN

FOR A SECOND or two, all I could do was stand rooted to the spot, staring blankly at Nick's broad back, narrow hips and long legs as he stalked off in the direction of the French doors that led from relative safety into wild wet mayhem. I was too busy reeling with astonishment to even think about formulating a response. And by the time it did occur to me to race after him and demand to know if he'd completely lost his mind, he'd flung open the doors as if the hounds of hell were at his heels and disappeared into the storm.

What on earth was going on? I wondered dazedly, my heart thundering as the doors slammed closed behind him. Was battling the horrendous weather really more appealing than answering my questions? Was his opinion of me genuinely that bad? And as for wanting to know why I cared what he thought of me, well, perhaps if and when he figured it out, he could let *me* know.

I got that my tirade had come out of the blue. It had taken even me by surprise—although all pressure cookers needed release at some point—so maybe it shouldn't have been that much of a shock. But why the sudden need to check out the generator? He'd only just declared such an act lunacy.

I couldn't unravel any of it. Everything was such a muddle. But really, only one thing mattered right now, and that was the fact that Nick had just taken leave of his senses and was now out there at the mercy of a savage mother nature.

What if something happened to him?

A dozen images slammed into my head then, tightening my chest and challenging my ability to breathe, but I ruthlessly shoved them away. I refused to contemplate a world without him in it. For better or worse—mostly worse, admittedly—he'd been part of my life for eighteen years, and things were just beginning to get interesting. But what could I do? I could hardly go after him. I had no choice but to trust that he knew what he was doing even though he'd looked and sounded as if he'd become unhinged.

The minutes dragged by like hours. I drank some water and ate a croissant. Outside, something creaked alarmingly. Somewhere inside the house, a door slammed. I discovered there was something to be said for pacing, and that the wringing of hands was actually a thing.

All I could think about was what might be happening outside and Nick's safe return from it. We hadn't cleared the air. There were things I needed to know and avenues I wanted to explore—the details of which were still unclear—but apart from all that, if something *did* happen to him, how would I tell his mother?

She'd made such sacrifices for him, her only son. She'd worked three jobs. And yes, he'd more than paid her back, buying her a house, and supporting her to retrain as a teacher, but she'd fought so hard, so tirelessly to give him a better future, and to have him perish so senselessly—

I didn't get to finish that thought. With a thunderous bang, the doors through which Nick had exited flew open. I leapt nearly a foot in the air and whirled around to find him striding back in. He was drenched from head to toe, the rain sluicing off him as he battled to close the doors behind him. His shirt was plastered to his body. His jeans had darkened to navy. A puddle was forming at his feet, but he was alive and looked to be in one piece, and the relief was so immense it nearly took out my knees before swiftly morphing into a tsunami of red-hot anger.

'Are you mad?' I yelled as I stalked towards him

on legs that were shaking so hard they were barely keeping me upright. 'What the hell were you *thinking*? How could you be so bloody irresponsible?'

'I needed some air,' he said, shoving a hand through his hair and dashing the water from his eyes.

Air? *Air?* Had he taken a blow to the head? Mine was about to explode. 'You said you weren't reckless but you could have been *killed*.'

'You care,' he said, stalking towards the downstairs bathroom, leaving a wet sandy trail in his wake. 'I'm touched.'

As I followed him, every cell of my body in turmoil, I didn't know whether I wanted to hug him or strangle him. Probably both. Because I cared more than I wanted to admit, which made no sense at all.

'You're definitely touched,' I said grimly, watching him grab a towel and rub it over his head. 'And to think I'm trusting you with my fortune. *I* must be mad.'

'We need power.'

'And do we have it?' I demanded. 'Because as far as I can tell the lights are still out.'

He tossed the towel onto the towel rail and strode past me. 'No. We don't. It would appear the problem with the generator isn't an easy fix.'

'So you risked your life for *nothing*.'

'Not for nothing,' he said flatly, heading for the staircase. 'For my sanity.'

'Your sanity? You must be joking.'

'I can't think of anything I find less amusing.'

'Am I honestly that bad? Were my questions really that difficult to answer?'

'You have no idea.'

'What does that mean?'

'Who knows? I sure as hell don't.'

'You're not making sense.'

'You're driving me insane.'

Ah, but he didn't know how worried I'd been. Even *I* had had no idea how worried I'd been. It was all very well for him to scowl and growl like this. He wasn't the one left behind to imagine the worst. 'If I am overreacting, it's because I was scared out of my wits.'

He stopped at the bottom of the stairs and turned to me, pinning me to the spot and stealing my breath with a look that was unsettlingly deep and searching, although marginally less fierce than before. 'Were you really worried about me?'

'Yes.'

'Why?'

There it was again. Another probing yet unanswerable question that sent me into a spin of confusion. I shifted my weight from one foot to the other, the sudden awkwardness awakening the jitters in my stomach and making me offer up the most superficial of explanations. 'Because if something had happened to you, what would have become of my money? Of me?'

His expression cleared and his mouth twisted. 'You've survived worse.'

Had I? Probably. Yet the dread that had mangled my guts was something I'd never experienced before and hoped never to experience again.

'And you'd soon find another financial advisor.'

'I don't want another financial advisor,' I said, recoiling at the thought of it. 'I want you.'

He gave a bitter laugh, which made no sense when he ought to be flattered that out of everyone on planet finance I'd chosen him, even if he was the best, but we were getting off track.

'At least you're back now,' I said, the panic and anger receding a little and some self-control returning as my racing pulse slowed. 'And by the looks of things, unharmed.'

'Sure.'

But as he put his hand on the handrail and turned to head on up, it struck me that something wasn't quite right. Despite the staircase rising up from the centre of the room, bannisters on both sides, he was using his left hand to hold on. In fact, come to think of it, he'd been using only his left hand since he'd stormed in from outside. And

now he had his back to me, I could make out a rip
in his shirt at his right shoulder and a darker stain
against the wet grey cotton.

'You're not unharmed, are you?' I said with a
lurch of my heart and a clench of my stomach.

He stilled on the first step. 'I'm fine.'

'What happened?'

'A loose roof tile. As I predicted. It's nothing.
Just a scratch.'

It wasn't just a scratch. Not if blood was seep-
ing through his shirt. But whatever it was, an inch
or two to the left and it could have been a whole
lot worse. 'You're incredibly lucky it missed your
head.'

'I don't know about that,' he muttered. 'It might
have knocked some sense into me.'

'Let me take a look.'

He turned an inch in my direction, his jaw tight
and a deep frown creasing his forehead. 'I said
it's fine.'

'It's not fine,' I countered. 'You're bleeding profusely.'

'Profusely is exaggerating it somewhat.'

'How do you know? You can't see it.'

'It'll stop soon enough.'

'There's no need to be stoical.'

'There's no need to make a fuss.'

A fuss? A *fuss*? 'You're being absurd.'

'I don't want you touching me.'

He made it sound like a fate worse than death and I flinched, each word piercing my chest. Whatever he'd claimed just before storming out, he really did find me horrible.

'I don't particularly want to touch you either,' I said, determinedly stamping out the tiny stabs of pain and lifting my chin and setting my jaw, because I was not letting this go. 'But the last thing either of us needs is for you to get an infection.'

For one long moment, I thought he was going to continue to resist. I could practically see the war against common sense raging inside him, but then he turned more fully towards me, the glare in his eyes abating a fraction, and, judging by the slight slackening of his muscles and the harsh exhale of his breath, appeared to relent. 'Fine.'

'Do you have a first-aid kit?'

'In the kitchen. In a cupboard, top left.'

'I'll go and get it. You sit down.'

Beyond relieved to have won *that* battle at least, I went to see what I could unearth. When I returned to the inner hall we'd been occupying earlier I found Nick sitting on one of the side tables, which he'd cleared of the lantern and pulled away from the wall. Pain was etched into his expression and I reckoned that had the lighting been better

I would have seen that beneath his tan he'd gone a little pale.

I set the first-aid kit down on the console table and moved to stand behind him. 'Take off your shirt.'

He tensed. I swallowed hard. Despite the chaos rampaging outside, everything seemed very quiet and still in here. Apart from my pulse. That was racing. And pounding in my ears. I'd never stood this close to him before. I'd never been so achingly aware of the parts of my own body that were responding to the proximity and heat of his.

It ought to have been a blessing that I couldn't see his face or watch him undoing his buttons, his long fingers deftly working the fastenings, inch upon inch of skin and muscle presumably being slowly revealed as he freed one and moved to the next. But it wasn't. Because my imagination was conjuring up the visual anyway.

Then he peeled back the sodden shirt, slowly, carefully stripping it from his right side first and then the left, and I didn't have to imagine. Right there in front of me was an expanse of smooth tanned skin that covered defined muscles I'd never have thought he could ever have possessed. The last time I'd seen his naked torso he'd been eighteen and lanky and storming off after I'd derisively told him he was beneath me. In the thirteen years since then he'd filled out. And *how* he'd filled out.

He leaned forwards, resting his elbows on his wet denim-clad thighs, and for a moment I just stared at the view, mesmerised by the way the flickering light of the lanterns cast dancing shadows over him and marvelling at the strength and power of his upper body. Until my gaze zoned in on the cut, which to my relief didn't look as bad as I'd feared, and I snapped out of my stupor.

I had to stop ogling. My hands were no use curled into fists, even if that way there was absolutely no danger I might reach out and stroke him. If I leaned in any closer—all the better to capture his mouth-watering scent—I ran the risk of toppling right on top of him and he hardly needed further injury.

Inhaling deeply for one last heady hit of salty sweat, tropical rain and pure masculinity, I pulled myself together. Nick was effectively my patient. It was my role to patch him up. I needed to concentrate.

'Be gentle with me.'

'I'll try,' I said, opening the box and extracting a bottle of alcohol, some of which I dabbed onto a wad of gauze. 'But this is going to sting regardless.'

I touched the gauze to the edge of the cut and he flinched. 'Sorry.'

'It's fine.'

'I'll be as quick as I can. At least it's stopped bleeding.'

'I told you "profusely" was an exaggeration.'

I resisted the urge to roll my eyes and focused instead on what I was doing. 'Once it's all cleaned up, I'll apply some antiseptic cream and then an adhesive dressing.'

'Look at you, Florence Nightingale.'

'I do have some uses.'

'Not just a pretty face.'

I froze. My pulse skipped a beat and then began to gallop. 'Sorry?'

'What?'

'Did you just call me pretty?'

'No. Ignore me,' he muttered. 'Come to think of it, I may well have suffered a bang to the head. I could have concussion.'

Ignore him? Like that was going to be possible. Whether he'd meant to or not, he'd paid me a compliment. Not a fact. An actual compliment. By his account, for the first time ever. It was dizzying stuff and bewildering as hell, and I wished I could see his expression and look into his eyes, no matter how unfathomable they might be, because what was going on?

'Keep still.'

'I'm not moving.'

Then maybe it was the room. Or me. My hands seemed to be trembling a little. My foundations were rocking. I couldn't quite believe that Nick Morgan, of all people, considered me pretty or understand why he'd chosen this moment to say it. *Was* he concussed?

Taking a deep steadying breath, I squeezed some antiseptic cream onto the wound and tried not to think about the fact that I was touching him, rubbing his lovely smooth skin in small slow hypnotic circles. About how easy it would be to stop rubbing and start caressing him with the whole of my hand, in larger circles that spread across the entire width of his shoulders and lower. About the hot heavy beat that was beginning to drum between my legs and how warm I was growing.

What would he think if I actually did it? I wondered, struggling to contain the urge to act on the impulses rising up inside me. What would he do? Would he leap away in horror or would he let me carry on? And if he didn't recoil in disgust, how far would he allow me to go? Could I run my fingers through his hair? Slide my hands around to his chest and press a kiss to the side of his neck?

Through the sluggish fog clouding my brain I heard him release a ragged breath, sensed something in his body give, as if a wave of defeat had washed over him, and saw him drop his head, chin to chest. 'Enough.'

'What?'

'I've had enough. I can't take this any more.'

'OK.' The fog pulverised, I whipped my hands off him, appalled by the suspicion that he thought I'd been groping him against his will. 'Sorry.'

'No. I don't mean the rubbing. You can carry on with that.'

My heart thudded. 'Then what do you mean?'

For the longest of moments he didn't reply. He sighed deeply again and shuddered, and then he said, 'Do you really want to know why I've kept my distance from you all these years?'

His voice was low. Gravelly. It skated over my nerve-endings and sent shivers down my spine, but at least it pulled me out of fantasy land and back to reality. The part of me that feared the shame of what he might reveal wanted to yell, 'No!' and retreat, but I located and clung onto the braver part of me, which was done with the antagonism and longed to correct whatever was wrong.

'I really do.'

'Do you remember what you were wearing the afternoon of your party by the pool?'

I picked up a cloth and frowned, the heat and the chaos swirling around inside me dissipating a little. What did that have to do with anything? 'No.'

'A pink bikini with tiny red strawberries all over it,' he said gruffly. 'A sheer white sarong tied at the waist. Your hair was held off your face with a pair of sunglasses and you were wearing a gold chain around your right ankle.'

My heart knocked against my ribs. 'That's a lot of detail.'

'I can recall all of it.'

'I'm not surprised.' The events of the afternoon had turned a relationship that hadn't even been a relationship into over a decade of icy hostility. I could recall quite a bit of it too. 'It was a memorable afternoon. Although not really in a good way.'

'I hadn't seen you for a while,' he said, the words slightly muffled by his chest. 'You'd grown up, and suddenly you were the sexiest thing I'd ever seen. I was dazzled. Instantly bowled over with lust. It knocked me for six, and I was still floundering when you sidled up to me and demanded I entertain you and your friends as if you owned me. Then you cut me down and it should have killed the attraction stone dead, but unfortunately it didn't. And that made me far more angry than your insult. How could I so badly want someone who thought so little of me? It made no sense. I had to stay away from you. For my own peace of mind. And since the attraction didn't fade, as I'd hoped, and you clearly didn't feel it too, I had to keep on staying away.'

He stopped and the silence that followed his words was immense and deafening. I was stunned. Speechless. Still wiping my fingers on the cloth even though the remnants of cream had to have been long since removed. I didn't know which bit to process first. The length of his speech? The fact that he'd once lusted after me and the implication that maybe he continued to do so? Or his misguided belief that I'd never found him attractive?

The shock of what he'd just said was too much to comprehend. Too huge. Only one of those clamouring questions could I even begin to address. However he'd felt about me before, he couldn't be attracted to me now. It was impossible. All evidence suggested the opposite.

And yet…

A montage of recent images and memories—from the afternoon I'd shown up here, then yesterday evening and this morning—broke through the dam of denial and flooded my head, suddenly pelting me with doubt.

What if the abruptness with which he'd dropped my hand after he'd helped me off the boat the day I arrived suggested the contact had had the same electrifying impact on him as it had on me? What if he'd frequently run his darkening gaze over me not to find something of which to disapprove but because he'd been unable to resist the temptation to check me out? Could the deterioration of his mood at supper last night have been a result of the battle he claimed to wage on the attraction he felt for me? And when he'd said half an hour ago we'd get through the storm by 'sitting it out', was the reason I'd got the impression he was envisaging something else entirely because he had been? And was that something the two of us in here whipping up a storm of our own?

Could I have been so blinded by my own hang-ups that I'd misread the evidence? It was entirely possible, I realised dazedly. To all those questions and suppositions, the answer could well be yes.

'Yesterday afternoon,' I said, suddenly desperate for confirmation one way or another. 'When I was talking about marine conservation, you were looking at my mouth.'

'I wanted it on mine,' he said hoarsely. 'I wanted it on me everywhere. I thought taking a cold shower while you were out on your walk would fix it, but it didn't. I thought thinking of you as a sister would help. But that didn't work either. I've never felt frustration like it. And the worst of it is, you are and have always been utterly oblivious.'

'But you go for leggy blondes,' I somehow managed, dizzy with shock and lust and who knew what else.

'Only to try and cure myself of an absurd fixation with a pint-sized brunette.'

'Five foot five isn't that short.'

'Every inch of you is perfect.'

My heart pounded. Who was this man? 'The day I arrived here you implied you couldn't wait to get rid of me.'

'I didn't trust myself to be alone with you. I was irritated for not having anticipated it and putting us in that position.'

'It was rude.'

'It was instinctive. It felt necessary. Self-preservation if you like.'

I knew all about that. 'You haven't exactly been friendly since.'

'As you keep pointing out—as if I need reminding—we aren't friends. But even if we were, it must be pretty bloody obvious by now that friendly is not how I feel about you.'

I swallowed hard. 'Why did you never say anything?'

'I'm not that much of a masochist.'

'So why are you telling me now?'

'Because I need it to stop,' he muttered darkly. 'It's been going on for far too long. I need to move on. I need you to laugh at me the way you did by the pool and tell me I never had a chance in hell and never will. And if not now, when we're stuck here with nowhere to go, then when?'

I could do that, I thought, my head spinning. I could easily do that. One quick scathing remark and that would be the end to this.

But I didn't want to.

And besides, it would be a lie.

I could no longer kid myself that the electricity and tension gripping my entire body were simply as a result of stress or meteorology playing havoc with my senses. Everything I'd thought incomprehensible, as transparent as mud, had become crystal clear.

The pieces of the puzzle had all fallen into place and I could now see that *this* was what the last thirteen years had been about. Despite my best efforts, I hadn't crushed the crush in the slightest. All along, behind the aloofness on his side and the hurt and frustration on mine, beneath the thick layer of icy hostility and forced civility, had been the simmering mutual attraction that had flared into life that afternoon by the pool and never gone away.

That had to be why I sometimes filled with the overwhelming urge to provoke a reaction from him. Why I'd never attempted to greet him with a kiss and had taken such care not to touch him all these years. Subconsciously I must have known it would all have lit a fire inside me that would have been impossible to extinguish.

So what was the point of pretending I didn't want Nick when it was blindingly obvious I did? Especially when, against all the odds, the feeling appeared to be reciprocated. I longed for his touch. I dreamed of his mouth. I'd become so practised at denying myself the good things in life—I'd had no choice—but I didn't have to deny this. I could have both his touch *and* his mouth. All I had to do was admit it, which wasn't a challenge at all.

'I can't do that,' I said, beyond desperate to find out what might happen next and willing to do anything to facilitate it.

He tensed. 'Why not? Does the thought of continuing to screw with my head amuse you that much?'

'God, no.'

'Then what are you saying?'

'I may not remember what *I* was wearing that afternoon by the pool,' I said, miraculously having the presence of mind to quit the cloth and rummage around in the kit for a dressing. 'But I remember what *you* were. A pair of black board shorts. That was it. You'd never really crossed my radar before. But my friends were talking about you and suddenly you did. You were all I could see. You sent me and my teenage hormones into a complete spin. I didn't take your rejection well and in my immaturity I lashed out. I spent the next three years partying hard in an attempt to eradicate the shame and shake my attraction to you.'

Silence. And then, a rough, 'Did you succeed?'

'I thought I had.'

'Thought?'

'I've recently had cause to revise my opinion.'

'What cause?'

My heart thudded. 'You want me to spell it out?'

'I want no more misunderstandings.'

Neither did I. 'I am far from oblivious of you, Nick,' I said as I applied the dressing with inconveniently shaking hands. 'When I look at you now, I get dizzy. When you look at me, I get hot. I keep having visions of kissing you. I keep seeing you naked. You have no idea of the things I've imagined this last week. Touching you like this is not enough. I want to touch you everywhere. But that would be inappropriate seeing as how you're all patched up and we're done.'

'It would not be inappropriate at all,' he said, his voice so low, so ragged it sent shivers down my spine. 'And you know something else?'

'What?'

'We are far from done.'

CHAPTER EIGHT

NICK WAS UP and on his feet before I'd had time to catch my breath, and for a moment, as he spun round to face me, all I could think was that his chest—broad, tanned, muscled, lightly dusted with hair—was far more magnificent than anything I'd been able to envisage.

'You want me,' he practically growled, his entire frame radiating heat and tension as he took a slow deliberate step towards me.

I lifted my gaze to his and stood my ground, my heart thundering, every cell of my body alive and quivering with anticipation. 'And you want me,' I replied since denial at this juncture seemed thoroughly pointless.

'So what are we going to do about it?'

It wasn't a question that required an answer, and I knew that he knew that I knew that. The next move was obvious and I ached for it so badly it bordered on agony, but he'd just been injured and it gave me pause for thought. 'I ought to say, nothing.'

His blazing eyes narrowed minutely and his jaw clenched. 'Nothing?'

'You're hurt.'

'You've patched me up.'

'You asked me to be gentle with you.'

'I've changed my mind.'

The intensity with which he was looking at me rocked the floor beneath my feet and obliterated my reservation. The fire in his eyes…it was like standing in a blast furnace. I'd wondered what I'd find if he ever lowered his guard, and now I knew. Focus. Intent. Desire, hotter and wilder than I could ever have imagined. All, unbelievably, aimed squarely at me.

'So what do *you* think we should do about it?' I asked, my nerves fizzing, my voice so throaty it was almost unrecognisable.

'What we should have done a decade ago.'

'And that is?'

His dark glittering gaze dropped to my mouth and my breath caught while my pulse raced. 'This.'

He took one final step towards me, reached out to pull me into his arms and slammed his mouth down on mine.

The kiss detonated a bundle of need inside me that then rushed through my body like fire. I whipped one arm up to his uninjured shoulder and around his neck and the other around his waist, finally touching him as I'd longed to, and it was electrifying.

Every inch of me was pressed up against every inch of him. He was strength and silk, power and heat, and I was drowning in sensation, in a kiss that was blowing my mind.

He tangled his fingers in my hair and angled my head, deepening the kiss with a skill and intent that made me moan. Heat poured through me as I kissed him back with equal hunger. He surrounded me. Enveloped me. He was all I could see and feel. My senses were swimming. The thick length of his erection, which pressed hard into my abdomen, triggered a persistent throbbing ache deep inside me.

I groaned as he wrenched his mouth from mine and set it to my neck. I instinctively dropped my head back to give him better access, a move he immediately took advantage of by taking his time to explore every inch of it before lingering on my pulse.

He slipped that hand that wasn't in my hair beneath the hem of my top, planting it at the base of my spine and pulling me tighter against him and I felt it like a brand. I ran my hands over his back, his chest, tracing rock-hard muscles with trembling fingers, thrills rippling through me, and all I could think, with my one remaining functional brain cell, was that this was Nick. *Nick*. Who I'd known for a total of eighteen years yet hadn't known at all.

How I'd once thought him cold and aloof was beyond comprehension. We were generating enough heat to fire a power station, more electricity than the national grid. This man wasn't staid and disapproving. This man was a volcano of heat and desire and for some unfathomable reason he wanted *me*.

In the midst of the storm raging inside me, I dimly heard a crack of lightning followed by a rumble of thunder and he broke away. With flattering urgency he backed me up against the console table and swept aside the snacks, the water bottles and the torches as if he didn't have a wounded shoulder or a thought in his head other than this.

Breathing so hard my lungs actually hurt, I pushed my leggings and pants down and off. Nick grappled with his belt and sodden jeans while I yanked my sweatshirt over my head, and then his mouth was on mine again and his hands were on the backs of my thighs. He lifted me up as if I weighed nothing and set me on the table. I parted my knees and he was instantly there, right where I was hot and aching and needed him desperately.

His hand cupped my heavy swollen breast and he rubbed a thumb over my nipple, which sent a sizzling shower of sparks shooting through me, but we'd had over a decade of foreplay. We had the rest of the storm to 'sit out' and take our time. Right now there was a mountain of pent-up lust to assuage, and I was going to explode if I didn't have him in the next thirty seconds.

'I need you inside me now,' I whimpered against his mouth, beginning to shake uncontrollably as desire continued to rip through me in ever stronger waves.

'I have no problem with that.'

He held my hips and tugged me forwards, while I spread my legs wide and wrapped my arms around his neck, and with one hard thrust he was buried inside me, so deeply, so fully, I actually saw stars.

For one staggering, heart-stopping moment neither of us moved. Neither of us even breathed. We just stared at each other, and I knew that the shock and disbelief that this was actually happening I could see in the swirling depths of his blazing eyes were reflected in mine.

Time seemed to stand still. All I could hear was my blood roaring in my ears. And as the seconds ticked by, my heart began to swell until it felt too big for my ribcage. My throat became so tight I couldn't speak. To my horror, my eyes started to sting. So I pulled his head down and slanted my mouth over his and, as I'd hoped, a wave of blistering heat swept away the strange surge of emotion.

Nick swore softly against my lips and held me in place and then, with a great shudder, began to move. Focusing entirely on the physical way he was making me feel, I wrapped my legs around his hips and, taking care not to dislodge the dressing I'd applied to his shoulder, clung onto him for dear life.

With every confident, powerful thrust, my senses shattered that little bit more. He was hitting a spot deep inside me with laser-like accuracy. He didn't need to be told. He didn't need reassurance. It was as if he knew me—or rather, my body— better than I knew it myself. All I had to do was go along for the roller coaster of a ride, hurtling through the sky-scraping ups and the stomach-disappearing downs.

When he sped things up, my head spun. When he slowed things right down, it spun even harder. My breasts rubbed against his chest, the friction charging me with a thousand volts, so I pressed closer and lost my mind. The disintegration of his breathing and the increasing wildness of his movements sent thrills shooting through me. My own breathing was harsh and desperate, my lungs capable of nothing more than short sharp pants.

Beneath my palms the muscles of his shoulders

and back bunched and flexed, the tension tightening them mirroring the unbearable tautening of mine. I felt feverish, fierce, desperate for something that was just out of reach. I wanted to bite him and taste him and do all sorts of wickedly wonderful things to him, but there was no time because, as if able to read my mind, he moved his hand from my hip to where we were joined, his fingers expertly finding my core, and within seconds I was coming so hard and fast I nearly blacked out.

The violent explosion that went off deep inside me flooded my whole body with wave upon wave of white-hot pleasure, racking me with shudders so intense I shook in his embrace. I wrenched my mouth from his, gasping for breath, while he pressed his face into my neck and surged into me one last time, hard and deep, letting out a rough groan as he found his own pulsating release.

His heart pounded against mine. His ragged breath burned my neck and his shoulders quaked. My limbs were weak. I felt boneless, as though I'd simply slither to the floor if he let me go. My mind was blitzed. I couldn't get over the fact that I'd just had the best sex of my life with a man I'd always thought I detested.

We stayed plastered up against each other for a moment, recovering from the cataclysmic encounter, but as our heart rates slowed and the sweat on my skin cooled, reality slunk in. The remnants of the heat and passion that had rocked my world a moment ago fled my body and awkwardness rushed in to take its place.

We were locked tightly together. I was naked. Nick's jeans were still open around his thighs. Supplies and my clothes were scattered across the floor. Where on earth did we go from here? Did we retreat to our corners to regroup and fortify our shattered defences or tumble onto the sofa for round two? What was there to say? He seemed to have no words and I was suddenly keen to fill the space.

'So that was unexpected,' I murmured, my voice raspy, my brain still trying to come to terms with the situation as I released my death grip on his shoulders and reluctantly removed my hands from his body.

He lifted his face from my neck, straightened a fraction, and stared at me, his eyes dazed, a dark flush streaking along his cheekbones. 'Was it?'

'Did you imagine it would be like that?'

'No,' he said with a slight shake of his head. 'I had no idea.'

'You sound awestruck.'

'I am. It surpassed my wildest dreams, and they've been pretty wild. You're astonishing.'

My chest gave an odd little squeeze, an after-shock of such mind-blowing pleasure, no doubt. 'You're the opposite of everything I thought you were. You're not cold. You're not aloof. You don't dislike me.'

'No.'

'I'd never have guessed.'

'That was the idea. Imagine the fun you'd have had mocking me. My ego wouldn't have been able to take the rejection.'

'I wouldn't have mocked. I'd have probably hurled myself into your arms. But I can see how you might think that. Sorry.'

'No,' he said with a quick shake of his head. 'If anyone needs to apologise, it's me. I went too far.'

A hot, apologetic Nick with the glimmer of sincerity and warmth in his eye was too much of a turnaround for me to process and I filled with an urgent need to get back onto more practical ground. 'How's your injury?'

'What injury?'

'Very funny.'

With the ghost of a smile, Nick rolled his shoulder and didn't even wince. 'It's fine.'

'Well, I'm not,' I murmured. 'I'm seizing up.'

He gently eased out of me and inched away and I missed his hardness and his heat immediately. I wanted to reach out and pull him back and forget myself, forget everything in more of his devastating kisses.

But he froze and frowned, and I shivered, an arrow of apprehension darting through me. 'What's wrong?'

'No condom.'

His words hit my brain like bullets, shattering the hazy afterglow with a brutal dose of reality. The implication of his realisation tilted the world on its access. My heart crashed against my ribs. My blood chilled. Protection hadn't even crossed my mind. We'd been so caught up in the rush. So frantic, so needy.

So careless.

'I can't believe I didn't think of it,' I said, a leap of alarm taking flight inside me even though there was zero point in panicking when it was far too late for regret and nothing could be done about it right now anyway. 'I *never* forget.'

Nick took a step back, then tugged his jeans up and refastened them, all traces of wildness and desire and humour gone. 'It's not your fault,' he said grimly. 'For the first time ever, I didn't think of it either. I was unable to think of anything, let alone get you upstairs to my room where there's a box. Are you on the pill?'

'No.' I slid off the console table and reached for my clothes with shaking fingers.

'Anything else?'

'No.'

He shoved his hands through his hair and then rubbed them over his face. 'Right.'

I slipped my top over my head and pulled on my pants and leggings, my stomach clenching and my heart pounding as I worked out the timeline. 'Date-wise, we could have a problem.'

'We won't have a problem.'

'What do you mean?' Could he somehow magic up some emergency contraception? Did he think that crossing fingers and hoping for the best actually worked? Or was he talking about abortion?

'If what we just did does turn out to have consequences,' he said, picking up his still damp shirt and frowning at it as if repelled by the thought of putting it back on, 'I'll take care of you.'

What?

It came as no surprise that Nick would want to do the supposedly right thing, and that was all well and good, but I hadn't spent years building up my self-reliance only to give it all up at the first hurdle. If, in nine months, a mini combined version of the two of us came along, I'd cope the way I'd learned to—by putting one foot in front of the other with my chin up and my jaw set, determined to look on the bright side. There was no guarantee he'd stick around—nobody ever did—and I wasn't about to put my faith in someone only to have them let me down by vanishing either physically or emotionally, or, quite possibly, both.

'There's no need for that,' I said, instinctively recoiling at the very idea of it. 'I have resources.' One hundred and eight million of them, in fact. 'I'll deal with it.'

'*We'll* deal with it.'

'At least it's not the nineteenth century, thank God. At least you don't have to marry me or anything if things do take a turn for the unexpected. Heaven forbid.'

He glanced up at me, his gaze dark and oddly unsettling. 'Do you have something against marriage?'

'You could say that.'

'What?'

I frowned. How was it important? Why did he want to know? And weren't we supposed to be focusing on the fact that we'd just had unprotected sex? 'We're drifting off topic,' I said, rather regretting the slip of the tongue.

'That horse has bolted,' he said and tossed the shirt onto the sofa. 'There's nothing we can do about it right now. Humour me.'

Yes, well, he might have a point about the bolting horse, but humour him? *That* wasn't going to happen. There was nothing remotely funny about the disintegration of my parents' marriage and the role I'd played in it, or its effect. My issues with trust and my insecurities over who I was and whether anyone would ever value me for me rather than what I did or didn't have weren't a source of amusement either. Besides, I never talked about my innermost hopes and fears. I had no one close enough to confide in and I wouldn't know how even if I wanted to, which I didn't, especially not now, when I was feeling so off kilter.

The sight of Nick's still bare chest and the memory of how it had felt plastered to mine mere moments ago were messing with my reason. I couldn't rid my head of an image of the hypothetical consequence of our moment of madness—a little boy with Nick's dark hair and my blue eyes, perhaps, or a little girl with my brunette waves and his cool grey gaze.

My initial panic at the thought of an accidental pregnancy had been instinctive, the result of social conditioning and ultra-stern lessons at school, but deep down I longed for a family and a place to belong. I dreamed of unconditional love and honesty, a future in which I could make up for the lack of both in my past. Deep down, I hated and regretted that I couldn't get over all the obstacles that prevented it.

The events of the last half an hour and the

thoughts streaming uncontrollably through my head now were making me feel confused and vulnerable in a way that I loathed when I'd fought so hard to be strong, and the need to protect myself by restoring my defences and keeping him at bay surged through me like a tidal wave.

'We had sex, Nick,' I said, ruthlessly burying the thoughts, the emotions and the images in order to regain control of myself. 'Long-overdue sex that's hopefully expunged the craziness from our systems, and great sex, I grant you, but that's all it was. It doesn't mean you can ask me personal questions. It certainly doesn't give you the right to dig around in my psyche. So back off.'

But if I'd hoped he'd take offence and storm off in much the same way he had earlier, the sharp shake of his head suggested I was to be disappointed.

'When we're finally getting somewhere?' he said, fixing me with a dark look that burned right through my skin and into my soul. 'Not a chance.'

In response to the glint in his eye and the determined set of his jaw, a tremor of alarm ran down my spine, followed hot on its heels by the need to set him straight. 'We're not getting anywhere.'

'What do you mean?'

'This—' I waved a hand between him and me and the console table around which the torches, bottles of water and snacks lay scattered '—was a one-off.'

'Are you sure about that?'

Of course I was. The part of my brain that was still drugged by the lingering memories of extraordinary pleasure and in need of another fix could forget it. Nick wasn't a random guy I met in a bar and took home for the night. He'd been part of my life for over half of it. We had history. He was way too disturbing to fool around with further. He had the potential to threaten the armour-plated sense of self-preservation I'd worked hard to achieve.

'One hundred per cent,' I said with a decisiveness designed to eradicate the sliver of regret that nevertheless shot through me. 'It was a brief, necessary release of tension. Nothing more.'

'What if I want more?'

What? My heart gave a slight lurch. 'Do you?'

'Yes,' he said, lifting his arms to fold them across his formidable chest.

'How much more? A day? A week? What?'

'More than you, by the sounds of things.'

'Well, *more* is never going to happen.'

His gaze sharpened. 'Never?'

OK, so that was a bit revealing. It was hard to stay focused when he was standing there in the dimly flickering lamplight naked from the waist up, like some sort of gorgeous demonic Greek god.

But I had to get a grip before I told him everything. 'I mean, not at the moment and definitely not with you.'

He frowned. 'Why not?'

'Because my life is too complicated and you're my brother's best friend.'

'So?'

'Imagine the awkwardness when things eventually fizzled out.'

'It would be no more awkward than the last thirteen years have been, and what makes you think it would fizzle out?'

'Neither of us has any experience of a proper long-term relationship,' I said, thinking of the way I never allowed anyone close enough to attach myself to them for anything longer than a week or two and his revolving blondes. 'My only one was a disaster and yours last no longer than a month. And then there's the fact that you're you and I'm me.'

'Which means what?'

'You're successful and brilliant. You know exactly who you are, where you belong and where you're going. I'm a failure and not brilliant at all. I don't have a clue who I am or where I belong or where I'm going. I grew up with everything, then had nothing and am now potentially on the way back to where I started. It's incredibly confusing. You're supremely sorted. I'm a basket case, riddled with hang-ups and issues. Quite apart from any-thing else, the differences between us are chasm-like.'

'That's ridiculous.'

Now it was my turn to fold my arms across my chest and arch an eyebrow. 'In what possible way?'

'You're not a failure. You've made the best of the hand you've been dealt and no doubt will continue to do so. Your intentions for your money are sen-sible. Your marine conservation plans are exciting and well thought through. You're gritty and deter-mined. Resilient and hard-working. The way you adapt to your circumstances is impressive, your relentless optimism is enviable and even though I didn't much appreciate the way you turned down my financial assistance all those years ago, I al-ways admired your pride.'

I stared at him, my jaw practically on the floor. He'd rendered me speechless. I couldn't even begin to formulate a response but that didn't matter be-cause he hadn't finished.

'Furthermore,' he continued before I could even think about swooning at his…what was that? Praise? 'I might know where I'm going and who I am, but sure as hell don't know where I belong.'

At that, my head spun even harder. He had to be joking. He was so self-assured. His confidence bordered on arrogance. I'd never met anyone more comfortable in their environment, whether having come from the office or out here in paradise. 'Seriously?'

He nodded, the fading light from the diminishing lanterns as they ran out of gas making it harder to work out his expression. 'Materially, I grew up with nothing. You know that. My friends back then had nothing either. All we had to look forward to was a future of yet more nothing. Then I went to that school where everyone oozed polish and confidence, where everything was possible and the future was for the taking. Even the sun seemed to shine more brightly. I was a fish out of water. I spoke differently. I dressed differently. And after I'd been there a while, the same was true when I went back home. I didn't fit in in my old world. I certainly didn't fit in in my new one where it was impossible to forget I was very much a charity case.'

The trace of bitterness I could hear in his voice tightened my chest. A charity case? I'd had no idea he'd felt it so keenly.

'You were an all-round star,' I said, suddenly burning with an unfathomable urge to redress the balance. 'You won every prize going, whether in the classroom or on the sports fields. That wasn't because anyone felt sorry for you. It was a very competitive environment. You weren't *allowed* to win. You just did. All the time. You completely deserved your place there. Far more than I did. I mean, let's be honest, it's not a coincidence that my father built the business centre the year I showed up.'

His brows snapped together. 'Do you really think that?'

'The evidence speaks for itself.'

'That's utter rubbish,' he said. 'You're one of the brightest people I know. You aced your exams and the university you went to only takes the best.'

'Ah yes, but who's to say my dad didn't pay for me to get in?'

'How can you think so little of yourself?'

I hadn't always. I'd brimmed with confidence once upon a time. But the shattering of my beliefs had led to a reassessment of everything and as a result I was permanently riddled with doubt. 'It's hard not to when people have always just sort of abandoned you.'

'What people?'

'My friends. My boyfriend at the time. My parents. They all disappeared in one way or another when the going got tough. There was clearly nothing about me personally that was worth hanging onto then. It's hard to believe that there might be now. Even Seb lives halfway across the world. All those adjectives you used to describe me—they aren't innate. I simply had no choice if I wanted to survive.'

'You underestimate yourself.'

'I don't. I know what I am,' I said, realising from the set of Nick's jaw—clearly outlined despite the dying light—that I wasn't going to win that particular argument and deciding it would be more worthwhile to redirect the conversation back to him. 'And if anyone's underestimating themselves it's you. Look at what you've achieved. Yes, you were given opportunities by others, but you made the most of them. Not everyone who went to that school did. One of my classmates even ended up in jail. You obviously inherited your mother's work ethic. Your success is wholly your own. If you truly have everything you could possibly need, then you more than deserve it.'

His gaze was intent on mine. 'I don't have *everything* I could possibly need.'

'No, well, everyone needs a place to belong.' I thought of the way he'd once wolfed down his food and the patched and darned second-hand uniform that had made him an easy target for the entitled jerks at school, of which I'd been one albeit without the bullying streak. And then I thought of the sports car, the confidence and the success, the custom-made suits and the watches, the penthouse apartments and the private tropical island we were stuck on. 'Although I must admit you seem very comfortable in the world you currently inhabit.'

'I enjoy the trappings that come with success, but I saw what happened to your father's businesses and the consequences of that. I take nothing for granted. I'm under no illusion I couldn't lose everything—' he snapped his fingers '—just like that.'

'That doesn't seem likely.' Nick had billions and he wasn't desperate to win back a wife who'd gone astray. 'By your own admission you're not reckless—what happened earlier with the generator notwithstanding—and you never let the personal interfere with the professional. And that's another reason for drawing a line under what just happened. We're in business together.'

'You're not an ordinary client.'

'Nothing about any of this is ordinary.'

'Least of all you,' he said, the certainty of his voice sending a brief dart of doubt arrowing through me that I batted aside because I'd had years to ruminate on everything and I knew what was what. 'Your inferiority complex is unnecessary, Amelia. Our so-called chasm-like differences are non-existent. You're using your brother as an excuse. He wouldn't give a toss what we got up to. And to hell with the personal-professional conflict of interest. I'm too good at my job for that to be a concern.' He took a purposeful step towards me and my heart began to race. 'You should know that I want to do what we just did again. Over and over again. We have years of wasted time to make up for and there are things I've imagined doing to you that would have you screaming with pleasure and begging for mercy.'

The heat that was now blazing in his eyes ignited a fire in the pit of my stomach quite suddenly, my head emptied of everything but one single thought. 'What things?'

Wicked wasn't a word that I'd have ever associated with Nick, yet it was the only way to describe the gleam that appeared in his eye and the smile that played at his mouth. 'I guess you'll never know.'

CHAPTER NINE

BEFORE I COULD give in to the insane yet impossible desire to demand detailed, physical clarification on the matter of *the things* when they were neither here nor there, I swiped a torch from the floor, turned it on and announced I was off for a shower. That it would be cold as a result of the power cut and the generator breakdown, which Nick pointed out, was not a problem. I was hot and sticky and desperately needed to cool off. I could only hope that there was enough water left in the tank to do the job properly.

Once in the relative sanctuary of the bathroom, I checked the window and the storm that was raging beyond. After a swift assessment that resulted in the conclusion that the risk of harm was minimal, I set the torch down and stripped off my clothes. I switched the tap to cold, then braced myself and stepped in.

But the shower wasn't the cooling, cleansing experience I'd been anticipating.

The minute I ducked beneath the flow of water—which, this being the tropics, wasn't nearly icy enough—it struck me that Nick's scent and his mark on me were sluicing off my body and being washed straight down the drain, and it felt strangely like a loss.

As I lathered up, the memory of his hands on me and the way he'd held me tight while he took me to the edge of the world and then hurled me over it slammed into my head and wouldn't budge.

When I ran the loofah over my abdomen, the sensitive skin there tingling and twitching, I found myself wondering what—if anything—was going on inside and what action I'd take in the event I made it to a pharmacy in time.

And then, as I stood rinsing off the bubbles, hoping to feel the zesty freshness my shower gel promised but instead feeling hotter and more skittish than ever, remnants of our conversation began to rattle round my head like the most fiendish of riddles.

Did he really not consider me a failure? Had he actually meant all those astonishing things he'd said about me? Could we be more alike than I realised and was it at all possible we had hang-ups about similar things? And why, oh, why could I not stop thinking about the nature of the things he'd said he wanted to do to me?

To my despair, my resolve to move on from what had happened on the console table was no match for my imagination. Vivid, erotic snapshots of the two of us together on a bed fogged my vision and muddled my head. The memory of the dark intent in his eyes made me tremble and shiver in a way that I simply couldn't stop.

In the days and months to come, would I always look at him and wonder, what if? Would I regret my decision to keep him at arm's length or find relief in it? Despite my concerted efforts to convince myself otherwise, deep down, I suspected I knew the answers to both those questions. Denial was hard to cling onto when the desire flooding my system was so insistent and refused to stay at bay. I wanted to know exactly how wild his wildest dreams had been. I yearned to feel his weight on top of me, pressing me down as he took what he wanted and made me scream as he'd promised.

By the time I switched off the water and stepped out of the shower I'd come to the conclusion that I'd overreacted by declaring fifteen minutes of passion a one-off. There was nothing momentous about what we'd done. People had spectacular sex all the time. I'd simply overanalysed the situation and got a little spooked. It had been so sudden. So unexpected. So unbelievably good.

But that was no reason to panic, I assured myself, rubbing my still tingling skin dry and slipping on my dressing gown as my pulse began to race. Scorchingly hot sex didn't have to mean anything. The *more* Nick had suggested he might want would never refer to an actual relationship, so, contrary to what I'd told myself earlier, he posed no threat to my defences. However good *the things* he'd imagined doing to me were, I certainly wasn't going to wind up weak, vulnerable and exposed to a whole lot of heartache when our relationship inevitably went wrong because we would never get to the relationship stage.

I'd let the shocking revelation about how he'd always wanted me, the abrupt reversal of everything I thought I'd known and the implications of a missing condom get the better of me. Once again I'd felt cornered and gone on the attack. But 'sitting out' the storm with him wouldn't be dangerous. We had to pass the time somehow, and probing conversation of the kind Nick had already attempted on a number of occasions, which might become increasingly harder to deflect if he kept up the pressure, didn't appeal in the slightest. Discovering what he wanted to do to me, however, did. A lot.

I was barely aware of picking up the torch and heading out of my room. The thundering of my heart drowned out my reason and my body seemed to have taken over. I felt as if I were floating as I went downstairs and searched the rooms, sweeping the bright beam of light around the spaces. Order had been restored to the inner hall where we'd made such a mess, I noticed, but of Nick there was no sign, so I went back upstairs.

I can't have knocked on the door when I reached his room. I must have simply walked straight on in. I had no hesitation in following the sound of running water. No qualms about slamming to a halt at the door that was ajar and staring transfixed at the reflection I could see in the full-length mirror that was in my line of sight.

Nick was in the shower, water pouring over his broad shoulders and the strong planes of his back, which was marred only by the square patch of the clearly waterproof dressing. He stood, legs apart, facing the controls. One hand was planted on the tiles high above his head, the other was wrapped around himself, moving up and down with quick, hard strokes.

My pulse hammered. My breath caught. Heat poured through me, charging along my veins and electrifying my nerves before pooling between my legs and throbbing deep inside. I couldn't move. My feet were glued to the floor. Wild horses couldn't have dragged me away even though I was invading his privacy in the most intimate way possible. I wanted to push open the shower room door, ditch my dressing gown and join him. I wanted to bat aside his hand, sink to my knees in front of him and drive him to completion myself.

But it was too late. His movements were becoming more frantic, less controlled. His jaw was tight and his muscles were straining. His raised arm was trembling. The hand on the wall clenched into a tight fist and then he let out a tortured groan. Great shudders racked his powerful body. His chest heaved as he fought for breath and shook.

The wave of lust that hit me like a torrent nearly took out my knees. I gasped, or maybe moaned, and it must have been loud and harsh enough for him to hear above the flow of water and the raging storm outside or maybe he suddenly caught a reflected flash of the torch beam, for he froze. He lifted his head and snapped it round. His gaze collided with mine in the mirror and for one agonising second neither of us moved. I was incapable of it. I was transfixed by the wildness of his expression. His eyes were dark and glazed. He looked savagely untamed and I shivered.

He switched off the tap and reached for a towel to wrap around his hips and disappeared from sight. Outside, the wind still howled and rain continued to batter the house. Inside, here, within me, the need to flee his understandable wrath at having such a private moment invaded warred with the urge to stay and achieve what I'd come to achieve, and I dithered, but a second later the decision was taken out of my hands.

Nick opened the door and leaned his uninjured shoulder against the frame, his laser-like gaze pinning me to the spot so fixedly I couldn't have moved even if I'd wanted to. 'Does it turn you on to watch?'

His voice was very low and it skittered across my skin, raising goosebumps all over me. I was so aroused, I was wet and aching and my knees were shaking. Five minutes ago I'd have said I didn't know if voyeurism was my thing. Now I knew differently. 'It certainly turns me on to watch you.'

'What are you doing in my room?'

I could hardly remember. Even my own name was a struggle to recall. But my hands itched to touch him. My mouth tingled at the thought of being crushed to his, and what I wanted flooded back on a wave of heat. 'I've changed my mind about our console-table encounter being a one-off.'

He arched one dark eyebrow. 'What happened to never again?'

'I panicked. I was in shock. I overreacted. But I was wrong. I must have been mad to think that once was enough after the build-up of all these years. I want more. I'm keen to know your every intention towards me.'

'My *every* intention?'

I nodded. 'I want you beneath me, above me, in every possible position. I need to know what these things you have in mind for me are. I want you to know the things I have in mind for you. And I'd far rather regret something I have done than something I haven't.'

He tilted his head, the intensity of his focus flipping my stomach. 'You'd regret it?'

Oops. Probably. But admitting to it might put him off, and that was the last thing I wanted. 'Only if it turns out to be mediocre, but I can't see that happening.'

'You still want me to be your plaything.'

I didn't know what I wanted him to be, other than naked and all over me. 'You give as good as you get,' I said, my heart beating hard and fast. 'Your "I guess you'll never know" was a deliberate taunt. You knew my imagination would go into overdrive.'

'And did it?'

'Yes.'

'God, you're dangerous.'

'Would you care to elaborate?'

'Not right now.' Nick pushed himself off the door frame, the set of his jaw, the intent in his gaze the most blazing I'd ever seen. 'Do you have anything on beneath that dressing gown?'

'Why don't you find out?'

He took the torch from my fingers and with one quick tug at the belt, one slide of his hands beneath the slippery fabric, Nick stripped the entire garment from my body. I gasped in shock and shivered, but not from cold.

'As I believe I pointed out this morning,' he murmured, drinking me in so intently I started to burn, 'every inch of you is perfect.'

I didn't know about that. My body was pretty average really, unlike his. I thought of him in the shower, the strong back and the long lean legs, all those lovely powerful muscles. Every inch of him truly was perfect, approximately nine of them, mouth-wateringly so. 'Likewise.'

I stared at his mouth, desperate for his kiss, and lifted my chin while I leaned towards him but he jerked his head back. A tiny chill rippled through me and with a frown, I froze. 'Games?'

He gave his head a minute shake. 'Payback.'

Before I could work out what he meant he'd pulled me into the shower room and moved behind me. He set my torch next to his on a shelf, angled me so we both faced the mirror and, after a moment, murmured, 'Now that's a view.'

I stared at my reflection. My cheeks were flushed, my eyes had darkened to indigo and a pulse hammered at the base of my neck. My nipples were tight and hard. Nick was a head taller than me and far broader and if he put his arms around me I'd be cocooned in heat and strength, but he didn't. Instead, he put his large warm hands on my shoulders and began to slide them down my arms.

He took my right hand in his and pressed it to the triangle of curls between my legs. The left he placed on my breast, and my entire body shuddered. I knew what he wanted me to do and I knew he wanted to watch. Nerves fluttered in the pit of my stomach. I'd never done anything like this before. It would have been way too sophisticated for the one and only relationship I'd had back when I was twenty and it was far too intimate for the casual flings I favoured nowadays.

In all honesty, it felt too intimate now, with the shadows dancing over the walls and us while outside the storm continued, but I couldn't have stopped even if I'd wanted to. The heat in his gaze was mesmerising and I was hypnotised. A sudden, unfamiliar but mighty wave of invincibility and power swept through me, filling me with strength and resolve. I wanted him to lose control the way I knew I was going to. I wanted him to beg for mercy. I wanted him to want me as much as I wanted him and for us to generate enough steam to power an engine. But there'd be time for that later. In the meantime, there was torture.

He released my hands but I kept them where they were. Locking eyes with him, I caressed my heavy, swollen left breast and rubbed my nipple, and had to bite my lip to contain my moan at the sensations that sizzled through me.

Without stopping, I instinctively widened my legs and between them, I stroked my fingers through the curls and the soft slick flesh until I found my core. I rubbed the hard, aching nub in small circles that stoked the need powering along my veins and made me tremble even harder. I was feverish. Electricity was zapping through me. Every nerve-ending I possessed was throbbing madly.

Behind me, Nick's jaw was tight and his breathing was becoming increasingly harsh and fast. He tore his gaze from mine and lowered it to my body and my hands, which made the desire shooting through me strengthen almost unbearably. He pulled me back against him and secured me there, his fingers digging into my hip, and I could feel the hard length of him pressing into me at the base of my spine. He swept my still damp hair to one side and set his mouth to my neck, branding my skin with a trail of scorching kisses.

On a shuddery exhale, dazedly wondering exactly who was torturing whom, I released my breast and lifted my arm to clamp my hand to his head. He slid his hand down my side and resumed the caressing, only it was so much better when he did it, and I arched my back to press my breast harder into his palm.

The tension building inside me was exquisite. The rush of anticipation and excitement was thrilling. My head spun and my breath quickened. I was so hot and my fingers were moving faster and harder, increasingly out of my control. The pleasure was rolling in and I closed my eyes and dropped my head back against his shoulder, a guttural moan sounding low in my throat.

Nick increased the pressure of his mouth on my neck and his hand on my breast and with one tiny pinch of my nipple, I was coming hard and breathlessly, spinning off into a splintering world of ecstasy where nothing existed but him and me and this.

I was still shaking and panting when I felt him scoop me up into his arms. My head continued to spin and my heart to pound as he carried me to the bed and dropped me in the middle of it. But when he ditched the towel wrapped around his hips and came down on top of me, the warm heavy weight of his naked body as delicious as I'd hoped, a fresh wave of desire gripped me and in an instant

I wanted him inside me with an urgency I could scarcely believe.

His head descended, his eyes as dark as the shadows all around, blocking out the flickering light of the lanterns that stood on the bedside tables, the room, everything but him, and I gave up thinking altogether and succumbed to the renewed sensations flowing through me.

His mouth fitted with mine so perfectly my chest ached. The kiss that followed was a hot languid exploration that went on for ever, not simply an entrée but a main event to be savoured.

I wound my arms around his neck and threaded my fingers through his hair and the growl that sounded low and rough in his throat vibrated against my lips and sent hot shivers down my spine. As the onslaught on my senses continued, the heat and need rising within, I writhed beneath him in a futile attempt to alleviate the growing pressure, but it only made things worse.

He pressed against me, now exactly where I wanted him. One tilt of the hips and he could be inside me, and I so badly needed that but he had other ideas. He took my wrists in his hands and pressed them to the mattress and set his mouth to the spot where my jaw met my neck. I dropped my head back and shivered at the sensations rippling through me.

He explored my throat with thorough and devastating care, and moved his mouth achingly slowly down my chest until he came to my breast. He captured my hot tight nipple between his lips and I would have jackknifed off the bed if he hadn't been pressing me down. I moaned, and he applied more pressure, his tongue driving me wild, and turned his attention to the other breast.

Too soon, he shifted down, dropping kisses down over my ribcage and my abdomen, the skin there jumping and twitching in response to the sparks he was generating and then he was pushing my knees apart and his mouth was there, on me, where my fingers had been only moments ago.

I was so sensitive it almost hurt but he knew exactly what he was doing. He read my body like a book. He licked me lightly and carefully and then, when my breaths shallowed and my moans deepened, with increasing intensity. I whimpered and clawed at the sheets and panted, the tension building while the ache deepened.

'Enough,' I breathed, grabbing his head and pulling him up. 'Enough.'

He kissed me, which made my head fog even more, then rolled away and sat up to rummage around in the drawer of the bedside table. Over the thundering of my heart I heard the crinkle of foil. I turned my head to see his shoulders were shaking as he applied the condom and I couldn't wait a moment longer, which he must have sensed because a second later, he was back above me, parting my legs and moving between them. He pushed into me, hard and deep and sure, and I completely lost what was left of my mind.

By the time Nick and I finally collapsed in an exhausted heap amidst the wreckage of his bed however many hours later, the wind had dropped and, although still squally, the rain wasn't hammering down quite so hard. When I eventually woke up the following morning, however, I saw through the balcony doors that the sea was now millpond flat, the palm trees were battered but still and the sky was once again a deep cerulean blue dotted with the odd scudding cloud.

I blinked at the warm sunshine streaming in and bathing the room in soft golden light and, with a wince, stretched. Every muscle in my body ached. I had stubble rash in places I hadn't thought it possible to have stubble rash. Nick had been true to his word. He'd made me scream. He'd had me begging for mercy on more than one occasion, and I'd returned the favour. We'd done things I'd never tried before but would definitely be adding to my previously limited repertoire. We'd only stopped to eat and rehydrate and refuel the lanterns as it began to get dark.

'Good morning,' came a gruff voice from the door to the bathroom.

I stilled mid-stretch and glanced over to find Nick standing there leaning against the frame with nothing on but some close-fitting underwear that left nothing to the imagination, looking at me in a way that made me shiver and ache suddenly in a different way. 'It's a very good morning.'

'Regrets?'

'None in the slightest. How's the shoulder?'

'Fine. Like I said, it's just a scratch.'

I rolled my eyes and grinned, which elicited a smile from him in return before he slid his gaze from mine to the view beyond the four walls of the room. 'The storm's over.'

'So I see.'

'I took another look at the generator. The power's back on. You can charge your phone.'

'I'm not sure I want to,' I said with a faint shudder at the thought of how many emails and missed calls I might have. 'Can you let Seb know we're OK?'

'Sure.'

'And the headlines? The photographers?'

'Gone.'

'Thank you.'

'So there's nothing to stop you from leaving.'

As his observation hung in the space between us, I realised with a disconcerting and unpleasant jolt that, theoretically, he was right. Not only had the threat of the press been neutralised, I'd also electronically signed the contract he'd emailed me while despairing about my response to him and fretting over the weather, so in that respect I'd achieved what I'd set out to achieve. The tension between us was history and we'd made a good start on clearing up all those misunderstandings. I could get up right now, put a call in to James and pack my things. I could be home in less than twenty-four hours.

But I couldn't think of anything I wanted to do less. I wasn't done here. Not by a long shot. Why on earth would I willingly give up the best sex of my life when it was still so new and exciting? Besides, the new level of understanding we were beginning to reach was fragile and needed further strengthening. Basically, this whole thing felt like unfinished business.

'Do you want me to?' I asked, my breath catching and my heart skipping a beat since it was impossible to tell from the look on his face what his opinion on the subject might be.

He shook his head. 'No.'

My lungs relaxed and warmth flooded through

me, the relief almost overwhelming. Thank goodness for that. I didn't need to stay long. I had a job and a life to get back to, a fortune to manage and a future to plan. So there'd be no danger of whatever was going on here turning into something more, of emotions becoming engaged or of me finding myself suddenly in too deep and unable to get out, as I'd feared only yesterday. There simply wouldn't be time.

'Well, I suppose I don't need to go just yet,' I said, my heart pounding wildly as, incredibly, desire began to drum through me all over again. 'As you pointed out, we have years to make up for. I can always get the morning-after pill flown over. And I do have a few days of leave left. It seems a shame to waste them, don't you think?'

'Good decision,' he practically growled as he slowly stalked towards me, weakening my muscles and melting my bones with his athletic grace and powerful intent. 'A truly excellent decision.'

CHAPTER TEN

IT WAS A good couple of hours before we resurfaced. When my stomach gave a rumble that put a stop to proceedings, Nick declared it was time for brunch and headed downstairs. I returned to my room to freshen up and to tease the knots out of my very tangled hair, which took quite a while given the mess he'd made of it. At the entrance to the kitchen, I gave him a twirl with a jazz hand 'ta-da' and he glanced up from the chopping board to give me a smile that stole the breath from my lungs and the wits from my head.

'If I'd known we were dressing up,' he said, evidently appreciating the one formal dress I'd packed judging by the heat in his gaze as it roamed over me, 'I'd have put on my tux.'

He didn't need a tux. He looked just fine in the pair of loose jogging pants he wore low on his hips. Better than fine. He looked good enough to eat but my body couldn't take any more and I was ravenous in a different way. 'You're funny.'

'I can be. You're stunning.'

'In this old thing?' I said, brushing aside the squeeze of my chest in response to his compliment and instead sidling towards him with a wave of one hand at the strapless pale pink sequinned bodice that flared out to a knee-length tulle skirt of the same colour. 'It's the only clean item of clothing I have left to wear.'

His eyebrows rose and his eyes darkened. 'Nothing else?'

'Nothing else.' Let him make of that what he wished. 'It's very liberating. Nice and airy.'

'Your clothes have always given me trouble,' he said, turning to the fridge and extracting a bowl. 'The image of you in that bikini stuck to my brain like a limpet. It didn't matter what you wore after that. I inevitably imagined you naked. It was immensely frustrating.'

'Am I meant to apologise?'

'You're meant to eat. You need to keep your strength up.'

I ignored the sizzle of heat that wound through me at that and the wonderment that we, who had been simmering and glaring at each other for years, were now flirting like pros, and instead eyed the smorgasbord before me. A plate of fat prawns surrounding a small bowl of aioli. Thick slices of crusty bread sitting between a pile of round juicy olives. Slices of cheese, miniature cucumbers and a stack of fragrant chicken skewers.

I hopped onto a stool, my mouth watering and my stomach giving another loud rumble. 'This looks delicious.'

'It's what I like to eat.'

'Is there anything you don't?'

'Potatoes,' he said, pushing a plate in my direction. 'I ate a lot of those as a kid. They remind me of being so hungry I hallucinated. I try to avoid them where possible.'

I pulled the plate towards me. 'What was it like?'

'Hasn't Seb filled you in?'

'I never really asked.'

'It wasn't much fun,' he said with what had to be a massive understatement as he rummaged in a drawer for cutlery. 'The village we lived in was badly deprived. The school was dismal and there wasn't a lot else to do. My mother was permanently exhausted. She worked her fingers to the bone but there was never enough money and never enough to eat. And it was always freezing.'

My heart gave a tiny, totally natural squeeze. 'Is that why you spend so much time here?'

'Yes. I hate the cold.'

'I can't begin to imagine.'

'And a good thing, too.'

He shut the drawer and turned to grab a couple of napkins and as he moved I noticed on the counter behind him a bottle of chilled champagne standing next to two cups of steaming coffee.

'What are we celebrating?' I asked. 'Off-the-charts chemistry? A truce?'

'Progress.'

I frowned at that, a ribbon of unease winding through me that I didn't think I could attribute to hunger. Where did he think this was going? Surely the sex and the flirting weren't giving him the wrong idea?

'Not *that* much progress has been made.'

'I disagree,' he said, handing me a knife and fork and a napkin. 'Look at where we are now compared to where we were yesterday. Imagine where we could be tomorrow.'

'We'll be right here,' I said pointedly. 'Right where we are. This is just sex, Nick.'

'There's no "just" about it.'

'You know what I mean.'

'I do,' he said and brought the cups of coffee to the island. 'But I don't think you quite understand the significance of what we're doing.'

I bristled and thought about stabbing something other than a piece of cheese with my fork. 'Are you patronising me?'

'Not at all. I'm simply streaks ahead of you.'

'I don't even know what that means.'

'Eat.'

Too baffled and annoyed to do anything else, I picked up a spoon and ladled some olives onto my plate, then added a couple of chicken skewers, only to pause when he suddenly said, 'Tell me something.'

I glanced at him and frowned. He was always trying to get me to tell him things one way or another, yet what could I do? Respond with a blunt 'no'? That wouldn't stop him. 'What?'

'That guy you were seeing at the time your father lost everything. Is that really the only relationship you've ever had?'

'Pretty much.'

'How come?'

'I have issues.'

'I thought we'd dealt with those.'

If only it were that simple. 'Different ones.'

'Which are?'

I tilted my head and narrowed my eyes at the man who was looking like the picture of casual interest as he started piling food onto a plate of his own. He was pushing me into another of those corners and the urge to go on the attack by deflecting the conversation reared up inside me. But this time, despite my irritation with him, something was stopping me following through on it.

I couldn't keep avoiding difficult conversation. Sooner or later, he would start to notice, perhaps to wonder why, and then push even more relentlessly for answers.

And perhaps it wouldn't be such a bad thing if I shared with him a thing or two. It might be uncharted territory but perhaps I ought to try and match his efforts to move on from the past and reach a plane on which we could peacefully co-exist. I hardly needed to go into detail. There'd be no need for an in-depth emotional analysis of anything. He'd been an on and off member of the audience at the show that was my life since I was eleven. He knew many of the facts already.

'My parents, for one thing.'

'What about them?'

'You can't have failed to notice their marriage was strained, even before my father lost everything.'

'I do recall a number of occasions when things seemed off,' he replied as he sat beside me, unnecessarily close, in my opinion. 'There was that fortnight we spent on the Amalfi Coast when she flew home early. Meals during which she barely said anything. Sometimes, I seem to remember, she looked downright miserable.'

'Things *were* off and she *was* miserable,' I said, burying the flurry of memories of the days spent diving with my father as we explored the coastal waters of the Tyrrhenian Sea, which had felt so special until they hadn't. 'She had an affair. That was why my dad screwed up with the money. He was trying to win her back and it made him desperate and careless.'

He turned his head and levelled me a look that had me feeling distinctly on edge. 'Is that it?' he said, his eyebrows lifting. 'Their example was a bad one so you've sworn off relationships for good?'

His scepticism raised my hackles, but my defences were indestructible on this. However hard he tried, he wasn't going to wheedle anything more out of me. There was carefully revealing a few minor elements of inner angst for the benefit of our future interactions and then there was the inconceivable baring of the soul. 'Isn't that enough?'

'No. I don't think it is.'

'Too bad.'

'Have you never been in love?'

I started and nearly choked on an olive. Nick? Talking about love? What was going on? 'Why on earth would you want to know a thing like that?' I asked, once I'd recovered from my coughing fit.

'I'm curious.'

'Have *you*?'

'Yes.'

He had no problem answering the question and it was on the tip of my tongue to ask who with but I bit the words back. It was irrelevant. None of my business. Furthermore, I didn't need to know. 'Are you still in love with them?'

'Yes.'

Oh. OK. That whipped the wind from my sails. 'Yet you're sleeping with me.'

'Now who's being judgemental?'

I frowned. He had a point. I had no reason to care. It wasn't my moral dilemma. Nevertheless, it was just as well I didn't want him for anything more than temporary excellent sex because if I had, I'd have been riddled with jealousy. But I didn't, so I wasn't. The tightness in my chest was a lingering effect of nearly choking on the olive, that was all.

'So what's your excuse?' I said, nevertheless keen to move away from that particular subject.

'What do you mean?'

'You're thirty-one. Rich. Successful. Hotter than the sun and not that deficient on the personality front, as it turns out. There has to be a reason why you're still single. An aversion to commitment, perhaps?'

'You're assuming it's me.'

I was. 'Isn't it?'

'I don't have an aversion to commitment.'

'The brevity of your affairs would suggest otherwise.'

'It doesn't suggest anything of the sort.'

'Then why have you never aimed for something more?'

'Maybe I'm working on it.'

Right. So was that why he'd been so keen to address the issues between us? Was he trying to get the overwhelming and inconvenient attraction he felt for me out of his system so he could move on to the woman he was in love with? Quite possibly. And that was completely fine.

'Well, personally,' I said, picking up a skewer and using my fork to push off the tiny chunks of fragrant chicken with a fraction more force than was possibly required. 'I never allow anyone close enough to get to that point. Like I said yesterday, people let me down. They disappear when they get to know the real me. I don't need that kind of hassle in my life.'

'That sounds lonely.'

It was sometimes, but it was a sacrifice I was more than willing to make. 'At least I stay safe and avoid any unnecessary pain,' I said as I dipped a piece of chicken into the aioli. 'And anyway, I don't think you're one to lecture on loneliness, when you're always out here on your own.'

'I'm not always out here on my own.'

That was a surprise, although I didn't know why I was so taken aback. Just because I had issues with other people it didn't mean everyone did. And the friction that existed between us could well be unique. He got on well enough with Seb, after all. And other women, one in particular it would appear.

'I'd have thought the blondes would burn,' I said a bit waspishly. 'The sun's very strong.'

'I wouldn't know,' he countered as he peeled a prawn. 'I've never brought any of them here. I was talking about my mother and her husband. Friends.'

Right. Well, that was something of a relief to know. But… 'But you have condoms. In a box. In your room.' And I remembered this, why?

'I picked them up at your hotel on Zanzibar.'

'So even in the midst of my misfortune, you were thinking of sex?'

His eyes darkened and his gaze dipped to my mouth and lingered. 'When it comes to you, I'm always thinking of sex. Among other things. Plus, I'm an optimist.'

Yes, well, no amount of optimism would get me back into bed right now, when I was hungry and feeling suddenly so out of sorts. And besides,

I was now curious about something else. 'What other things?'

'You don't want to know.'

'That bad?'

He thought for a moment, then eventually said, 'Over the years, you've meant chaos and disruption. Monumental upheaval and a constant battle for control. Stress and frustration and endless cold showers. I've resented you for having that effect on me. I've despised myself for not being able to conquer it.'

So it was that bad. I should never have asked. 'And now?'

'You still mean all those things.'

'No wonder you described me as dangerous,' I said lightly while feeling, of all unexpected things, a little upset.

'Don't forget gritty, hard-working and optimistic.'

'Not to mention resilient and determined.' Currently being demonstrated by my resolve to get over myself. 'And there was me thinking you'd always considered me impossibly silly and superficial.'

'Not for a long time.'

I leaned back and stared at him in surprise. 'Really?'

'You may have had your moments when you

were younger,' he said, 'but underneath it all you were…kind.'

I blinked. Of all the adjectives he could have chosen after describing my more destructive qualities, that was not one I'd ever have considered. 'Kind?'

'You were forever finding small injured animals and taking them in. Frogs. Squabs. Bumble bees. If it was missing a wing or had fallen out of a nest it had to be saved.'

'I'd forgotten that,' I said, slightly taken aback that he remembered. 'I didn't always succeed.'

'But you always tried. You fought for the weak. You championed the underdog. Do you recall coming to my defence once, when some kids at school were taunting me about where I was spending the holidays? I was handling things fine on my own, but that didn't stop you flying into the melee and telling everyone exactly what you thought of them. You were small but fierce. Like a mini Boadicea. I was impressed.'

I searched my memory, but it didn't take long. 'I do remember,' I said, thinking that was one moment involving him that I could be proud of at least. 'I was eleven to your thirteen. It was the end of your first term and I was with my parents, picking Seb up. You and I hadn't met at that point. I just saw injustice and reacted. But if I'd known how disruptive and unwelcome you were going to find me,' I added a touch tartly, 'I might not have bothered.'

'I'm glad you did.'

When had I lost that fearlessness? I wondered, mopping up the juices on my plate with some bread. When did I stop caring about those in need of help? When did I become more interested in clothes and make-up and a bunch of pretty rotten friends?

'Do you know what you also were?'

I snapped myself out of my turbulent thoughts and refocused. 'I'm not sure I want to.'

'You were influential.'

My eyebrows shot up. 'Influential?' That was an improvement on resented and chaotic, although it could hardly have been any worse.

'Firstly, if it wasn't for you and the conversation we once had about it, I'd still be messed up about having a father I've never met. I'd still be feeling guilty about spending so much time with your family instead of my mother. And secondly, without you I wouldn't be who I am today. Your comment about me being beneath you—' He broke off, a flare of heat lighting the depths of his eyes and I went hot, despite the lingering pique at the knowledge he'd found me so impossibly frustrating. 'It sparked my drive to succeed. To make money. To be and do better than everyone else. I admit there was the money element. I wanted to get my mother and myself as far away from where we came from as possible. I swore to myself that neither of us would ever be hungry or cold again and didn't stop until I achieved that. But I was initially driven by you and your disdain. That's why I've never needed or wanted your apology for that afternoon by the pool, Millie. If anything, I ought to thank you.'

Nick fell silent but the noise in my head was deafening. I was, in part, responsible for the man he'd become? My adolescent petulance had led to his stellar success? I didn't know whether to be ashamed of that or proud. I didn't know what to think any more. I went from hot to cold and back again. I was influential and chaotic, annoying and Boadicea, resented yet desired.

But suddenly none of that seemed to matter. It was all swept aside by the Millie. He hadn't called me Amelia. He'd called me Millie. For the first time ever. Which, for some bizarre reason, had my heart flipping about all over the place, an unstoppable smile curving my mouth, and all my outrage and pique, my objections and concerns melting clean away.

'You're welcome.'

After brunch, we ventured outside to inspect the storm damage. The ground was waterlogged.

Leaves and branches lay scattered everywhere and the flowers in the planters were trashed. Much of the debris had ended up in the pool and I spent a good quarter of an hour watching and admiring as a shirtless Nick scooped it out, which eventually led to a scorching interlude on a sun lounger.

Later, once we'd cleared up the worst of mother nature's fury in the immediate vicinity of the villa, he grabbed my hand and led me down the path to the jetty, which remarkably remained intact. He dragged the boat from its shelter with an impressive display of muscles and fired it up, and ten minutes later we were motoring around the island to check on the rest of it.

The beach at the cove I'd explored yesterday lay beneath half a dozen felled palm trees, their freshly jagged trunks jutting out of the churned-up sand. The door to the boathouse at the top end of the island was hanging off its hinges and as Nick steered the boat into the shore I could see that the sails had been blown off the walls and the kayaks and boards had slipped from their supports.

The devastation that lay all around was a side to paradise that didn't appear in the brochures— and I didn't dare imagine what it would have been like had the storm been stronger and lasted longer—yet it occurred to me as Nick cut the engine and jumped off the boat into the once limpid but now murky shallows that, extraordinarily, out of it, in our tiny corner of it, at least, had come harmony.

Because of it, we'd been forced to confront our history. We'd cleared up the torturous past and paved the way for a smoother future. And while he'd frequently tied me in metaphorical knots, which had hampered clarity on certain subjects somewhat, there'd been honesty.

Best of all, it hadn't been as bad as I'd feared. I hadn't been forced to disclose anything particularly deep or shameful. I wasn't overexposed and emotionally vulnerable. In fact, if anyone had been revealing, it was Nick with the 'Millie' that perhaps proved he no longer considered me quite such a disturbing nuisance these days.

'You're very quiet,' said Nick, jolting me out of my reverie and drawing my attention to the fact that while I'd been wool-gathering he'd pulled the boat up onto the sand and unloaded bits of the kit he'd randomly accumulated earlier, just in case.

I stood up and smoothed my dress, only to have to do it again after he'd planted his hands on my waist, lifted me off the boat and let me slide down his body as he lowered me to the sand. 'I've been thinking it feels as if we're in some sort of parallel universe,' I said, a little breathless after the gallantry that hadn't been necessary but was deliciously thrilling all the same.

'In what way?'

'You and me working together and not glowering at each other, for one thing.'

He handed me a drill and an electric screwdriver then loaded himself up with rope, a couple of planks of wood and the toolbox. 'It does make a change.'

'I can't envisage you in a suit any more,' I said, running my gaze over his tousled hair, the reflective sunglasses that glinted in the sun and the shorts that this afternoon were electric blue with white stars. 'Or in an office. It's all very weird.'

'It's progress.'

Well, yes, I thought as I followed him up the beach to the boathouse and mulled it over. I supposed it was in a way, although, worthy of a champagne celebration? I wasn't so sure. 'Do you ever wonder what things could have been like between us if you'd done them differently?'

Nick dumped everything he was carrying on the deck, lifted his sunglasses to the top of his head and narrowed his eyes as he inspected the damage. 'Frequently.'

'If I'd swallowed my pride and accepted the money you offered me,' I said, adding the drill and the screwdriver to the pile, 'I would probably have finished my studies. I might have pursued a career in marine conservation and already have achieved everything I want to for the turtles.'

'You wouldn't have had to live in a flat share and survive on soup.'

'True,' I said with a tilt of the head. 'But I'd still have resented you for it, I suspect. And it's not been so bad really. I've lived the last eight years on my own terms and I know I can rely on myself and there's value in that.'

Nick picked up a plank and a hammer and handed me a box of nails. 'You can rely on me.'

Could I? Who knew? As the terms and conditions of our contract stated, past performance was no guarantee of future results. 'I prefer not to.'

'I know.' He lifted the plank into the space where one was missing and gestured to me to hold up one end of it. 'It's disappointing.'

I held out the box of nails and he extracted two. 'It's nothing personal.'

'It feels pretty personal.'

An incomprehensible surge of shame and regret swept through me then, but I pushed it back down because there was no reason to feel either. 'So what would you have done differently in this parallel universe I'm imagining?'

'I'd have let your comments that afternoon at

your pool slide,' he said, banging in the nails and reaching out for more, which I duly furnished him with. 'We'd have ended up in bed a whole lot sooner than yesterday and wasted a lot less time.'

'But it would still have been just sex and it still wouldn't have lasted.'

'It would have lasted a damn sight longer than the couple of days you've set aside for it, trust me.'

'But you see, that's exactly the problem.'

Nick paused, hammer aloft, and looked at me quizzically. 'What is?'

'Trust.'

He frowned. 'You said you trusted me.'

I stared at him. 'When?'

'Yesterday. When I asked you if you thought it was me who leaked your news to the press.'

Ah. 'I said I trusted you with my money.'

His eyebrows lifted. 'And that's it?'

I nodded. 'That's it. I don't trust anyone. I want to, somehow, but I can't. It's simply too ingrained. An impossible habit to break, if you like.'

'Stemming from everyone abandoning you at a time you needed them most?'

'Quite.'

'That's understandable,' he said, and stood back to admire his handiwork. 'But I disagree about it being an impossible habit to break. Trust is a choice.'

'That's easy for you to say,' I said, annoyed at the way he was so casually brushing aside something that I felt so deeply. 'You haven't been let down by virtually everyone who's supposed to be on your side.'

'I'm on your side and I haven't let you down.'

'It would only be a matter of time.'

He turned to me, the intensity in his gaze nearly taking out my knees. 'Do you really believe that?'

'Yes. Why?'

'I assumed you thought more of me.'

'I don't think anything of you,' I said, stifling a sigh of exasperation. 'That isn't what this is about. I keep telling you that.'

'You keep telling yourself that.'

What did that mean? That he knew me better than I knew myself? That was a bit presumptuous. 'Anyway,' I said, moving on from irritating observations that were too cryptic to work out, 'don't you ever worry that your friends like you only for your money?'

'No.'

'Well, I do,' I said, as he turned his attention to the door. 'After what happened before, I'm petrified I'll make bad choices again. I still can't quite bring myself to believe one hundred per cent in people's motivations. It's even more of a concern now that I have all this money.'

'So why play the lottery?'

'Because I wanted a little bit of what I once had,' I said a tad wistfully. 'I wanted to be able to spend money without worrying about it. And there are things I miss. Like fresh flowers and amazing food. Not even having to think about bills. I never really expected to win, certainly not the amount I did. I realise that my complaints are very much of the "my diamond shoes are too tight" variety but the responsibility is immense and, frankly, terrifying. When I think of how close I came to losing it my blood runs cold.'

'Don't blame yourself for being susceptible,' he said, retrieving a ladder from the boathouse and propping it up against the side of the building. 'It happens.'

'I bet it doesn't happen to you.'

'You'd be surprised.'

I watched him pick up the electric screwdriver and refix the door to the hinges with unexpectedly attractive competence and thought of his strength, his self-assurance, his drive to succeed and his single-minded focus. He might have issues about his place in the world but, presumably, one didn't rise from nothing to become a billionaire businessman without a little bit of ruthlessness and a whole lot of savvy. The idea of him being susceptible to anything in any conceivable way was laughable. 'I would indeed.'

CHAPTER ELEVEN

HAVING REPAIRED THE damaged building the best we could with the limited kit we had, Nick and I returned to the boat and loaded it back up. While he opened the throttle and steered in the direction of the longer western coast of the island, I closed my eyes, sat back and lifted my face to the breeze.

But it wasn't as relaxing an experience as I might have been forgiven for thinking it would be. The conversations we'd had today kept spinning round my head and with every passing minute the unsettling sense of foreboding winding through my body was strengthening. I was feeling increasingly on edge and jittery, untethered and at sea metaphorically as I was literally.

I didn't like the way he said things that I simply couldn't work out or that he constantly seemed to think he knew something I didn't. The fact that the only area in which we were on the same page was sex worried me but not as much as the realisation that, despite my concerted efforts to keep what was going on strictly physical, I wanted to cross the line into the personal.

I wanted to know everything about him. The big things and the small. His hopes, his fears, his dreams. I wanted to know what his favourite colour was. His musical tastes. More about his background, which had to have been so formative, and where he really hoped he'd be in five years' time. I didn't want to leave Suza until I knew it all. I didn't much want to leave at all.

The trouble was, he was so much more complicated and layered than I could ever have imagined. So much more interesting and compelling and surprising.

Take the talking that had been going on. When I'd first met him, he'd been adolescently sullen. For years, we'd exchanged the most cursory of words. But not any longer. I'd learned more about him in the past week or so than I had in eighteen years and whereas, only ten days ago, he'd stared at me in horror at the mere hint of tears and I'd been convinced that his was not a shoulder to cry on, I now had the feeling that perhaps it was.

And none of this was good.

I didn't need to know any of the things I longed to know. My heartstrings shouldn't have been tugged by his brief revelations about his upbringing. I had no business wondering what it might be like to have him truly on my side, to be loved by him. The way he'd corrected my chronically low self-esteem in so many different ways shouldn't mean anything. I oughtn't to care about the fact that he'd seemed gutted by my revelation that I couldn't rely on him and would never trust him.

This wasn't some great sweeping romance where everyone sailed off into the sunset and lived happily ever after. This was simply an attempt to examine the past, work through misunderstandings and address the unacceptable and intolerable tension so we could move forward, while having some seriously fantastic sex. Yet I was in danger of losing sight of this.

I was normally so level-headed, so sensible, but around him I behaved completely irrationally. Since my return to Suza, I'd allowed him to push and challenge me. I'd talked to him, with barely a moment's hesitation, and while I'd just about managed to keep my deepest secrets to myself, I'd told him enough.

I was out of control and it had to stop. What we'd been doing didn't feel thrilling any more. It felt impossibly dangerous. If we continued with this even a day or two longer, I could see myself falling further under his spell, further into a deepening pit from which there'd be no escape. I might start craving conversation, seeking his opinion and wanting that shoulder to cry on. I might share with him the conflicting feelings I had about my father, the sorrow and regret I felt about being too afraid to let anyone close. And if I did, I'd be barrelling down a path that would only lead to more pain when he left, which everyone did, one way or another.

I should never have given into temptation and stayed. I should have paid attention to the warning signs, of which there'd been many. But it wasn't too late to rectify the situation. The clarity of my mind and the strength of my resolve were matched only by my desperate need for self-preservation.

After disembarking I strode up the jetty, aware that Nick was hot on my heels. He took my elbow and steered me towards a sofa upon which I knew he intended to take me to heaven and rob me of my wits. But that couldn't happen so I shook myself free and headed for the stairs instead.

'Where are you going?' he said, capturing my wrist and drawing me so close that for the briefest of seconds I wondered what on earth I was thinking by intending to give up this crazy hot desire.

But it was precisely because of the ease with which he made me lose my reason, my control, that I needed to stick to the plan. So I pulled away, smoothed my dress, and from a safe distance said, 'To my room.'

'Why?'

'I need to pack.'

He froze at that, a frown creasing his brow, bewilderment flickering across his face. '*Now* you want to leave?'

'Yes.'

'Why?'

'There's no reason not to,' I said, holding at bay all the arguments that countered this. 'Thanks to you, the press has retreated. We've expelled the lust from our system and sorted out our differences, which bodes well for future encounters. There are things back home I need to be getting on with and I have a job to return to, not to mention a pharmacy to visit.'

'What's going on?'

'I thought we were on the same page but we clearly aren't. So I need to go.'

'I'd like you to stay.'

Well, that was just tough, I thought with a firm shake of my head, as much to convince myself of my resolve as him. 'This fling of ours has been a lot of fun, Nick, but it's over.'

'It isn't a fling,' he said, the intensity in his gaze for some reason triggering flutters in my stomach and accelerating my pulse. 'At least not for me.'

'What are you talking about?'

'I'm in love with you.'

In response to Nick's startling declaration, my heart gave a great lurch and then began to pound, the only sound in an otherwise dead silent room.

'What did you say?'

'You heard. I'm in love with you.'

I frowned, confusion lancing through me. What on earth was he talking about? Had the hot blazing sun yesterday gone to his head?

'That's ridiculous,' I said, even more at sea than I'd been fifteen minutes ago. 'Why would you say such a thing?'

'Because it's true.'

'After two days?'

'No, Millie. I've been in love with you for years. Probably in some shape or form ever since you flung your fists around in my defence as a fearless and feisty eleven-year-old.'

What? 'Years?' I echoed faintly. 'But you've been paving the way for someone else.'

'Someone else?'

'When we were talking about the brevity of your relationships and I asked you why, if you didn't have a problem with commitment, you didn't seek something more, you said you were working on it.'

'Yes. But not someone else. You. I've been working on you. Last night, you asked me what the one thing I wanted but didn't have was,' he said, the steadiness of his voice and his air of absolute calm a complete contrast to my bewildered thoughts. 'Well, it's you. The reason I've never committed to anyone is because the only person I want to commit to is you. I want to marry you, Millie. I want to have a family with you. I want everything with you. You asked me once where I saw myself in five years' time. I see myself with you. With a child that we may or may not have already created. Maybe two. What am I afraid of? That it'll never happen.'

He stopped, clearly waiting for some kind of response from me but I didn't have one. My mind had gone blank. I didn't know what to say. I could scarcely breathe. How on earth could he be in love with me? It made no sense at all. He had to be joking. But he didn't look as if he were joking. He was as serious as I'd ever seen him and as it hit me that he really believed what he as saying, deep inside I could feel the stirrings of panic.

'I think you're confusing love with lust,' I said, my stomach beginning to churn violently.

'Believe me, I am not. I know the difference. I've done things for you it wouldn't even occur to me to do for anyone else. I've pulled you out of bars when it was anything but convenient. I've looked out for you and not just because your brother asked me to when he left for the States. I offered you that money not out of pity or charity but because I couldn't stand the thought of you suffering any more than you already had. You pointed out that whenever I walk into a bar I look around as if in search of someone. That someone is you. Your welfare is all that's ever mattered to me. That's why I came to pick you up on Zanzibar. That's why I shut down the press. I did all of it for you. Only you.'

'But you find me chaotic and disruptive,' I said, every bone in my body, every stunned cell in my brain rejecting what he was saying.

'And beautiful and strong and brilliant. I always have. Even when you were telling me I was beneath you and throwing my money back at me. I've been trying to tell you how I feel about you, to show you, and I hoped I'd have more time, but if you're really going to leave then I'm done with subtlety. I'm done hiding. We've wasted too much time already and after the last twenty-four hours, I don't think I could stand a return to the way things were before. I know you have a problem trusting people. I know you're afraid of being let down. I know you doubt people's motivations, but you can trust mine and you can trust me. I will never let you down. Let me love you. Love me back.'

This was all too much. The pressure bearing down on me was crushing the breath from my lungs and draining the blood from my head. My defences were under such heavy assault they could buckle at any moment, but for now they were still intact, thank God, and I had to take strength from that. I had to use them to quash my weaknesses, to bury my vulnerabilities and above all to protect my heart.

'I can't,' I said, suddenly seeing things very calmly and very clearly.

'You can.'

'I thought you were the one person who had never lied to me, Nick, but you've been knowingly lying to me all along. You say you've loved me for years but for years you let me think the opposite. I understand your reasons for it, but you treated me horribly. With the impression you gave of disdain and disapproval you made me feel even more worthless than I already did. You hurt me.'

He flinched as if I'd slapped him and went white beneath his tan. 'I didn't know that.'

'For me, what we've been doing has always been a short-term thing. It's all it ever could be. I never asked you to fall in love with me. I never wanted it. I certainly don't deserve it.'

'You do. Everyone does.'

Not me. 'You couldn't possibly understand.'

'Then explain it to me.'

'I have nothing to offer and I can't be responsible for other people's happiness,' I said, my throat tight, my heart beating impossibly fast. 'The breakdown of my parents' marriage. The affair. Our misfortune. My father's heart attack. It was all because of me.'

'What the hell are you talking about?'

'My father and I were like two peas in a pod. Right from the start, we were close. Really close. On reflection, exclusively so, sometimes. Maybe it was because I looked so like him. I don't know. But Seb told me once that my mother had told him she felt invisible and neglected. She admitted to him that she was jealous of our bond. I'm the reason she had the affair. I'm the reason my dad tried to win her back and lost everything in the process. It's all my fault.'

'That's insane.'

'It's easy for you to say. You don't have to live with it. Regret doesn't constantly hover around the edges of your conscience. Guilt and shame don't niggle away at you day and night. You weren't there. I was. I know what happened.'

'You know what you think happened.'

I bristled. 'What does that mean?'

'I know your mother regrets your estrangement. I know she can't understand it.'

'How?'

'She and my mother talk from time to time. They discuss us.'

Us? There was no 'us'. I could never be part of an 'us'. And how on earth could my mother not understand the reason we barely spoke? I'd ruined their marriage. Wasn't it obvious? 'It's not her fault.'

'It's certainly not yours. If anyone it's your father's. It was his marriage to ruin and he was no saint.'

What did *that* mean? 'Yes, well, he's not around to ask, is he?'

'I think you're using it as an excuse,' said Nick, not quite so steady now, not quite so calm. 'I think you're scared.'

'Of course I'm scared. I'm terrified. Why do you think I haven't had a long-term relationship since my one pathetic boyfriend ghosted me the minute I became penniless? I've spent years building up my defences to protect myself against hurt and to become as invincible as I can possibly be. To let no one close enough to threaten that. I'm not going to throw it all away just because you claim to be in love with me.'

'It's more than a claim.'

'So you say.'

'You called *me* from Zanzibar.'

'Because there was no one else.'

The tension throbbed between us. Then Nick shoved his hands through his hair and rubbed them over his face.

'You know what?' he said, resigned, defeated, hollowed out. 'Fine. Have it your way. Be obstinate. Stick your head in the sand. I've waited for you for years, Millie. I've been tormented by you and wanted you and loved you for years. I had hoped that at some point you'd come to realise you feel the same way.'

'I don't.'

'I get it. Believe me, you've made yourself perfectly clear. So enough. We're done. Go ahead. Pack up your things. I'll take you to the airport myself.'

As I could have predicted, the boat ride to Dar es Salaam was horribly awkward and uncomfortable. Neither of us had anything to say, not even a comment about the stunning sunset. Nick stood at the helm, staring resolutely ahead, lost in thought, while I sat to his left, the wind whipping through my hair as I counted down the minutes to my departure.

I'd done absolutely the right thing in setting him

straight on the situation, I assured myself repeatedly as the boat ate up the nautical miles. I had nothing to feel guilty about. It wasn't my fault he fancied himself in love with me. He'd soon come to realise he was mistaken and then he'd be amazed he'd ever thought it in the first place. The memories of my time here would fade eventually. By the time we next met, it would be as if none of this had happened.

'One thing before you go,' he said, once he'd offloaded my suitcase into the car that was waiting at the quayside.

'Yes?' I said, bracing myself for more revelations I didn't want and would never be ready for.

'I apologise for the way I've made you feel all this time. If I'd known... Well.' He shoved his hands through his hair then stuck them in the pockets of his jeans, swallowing with apparent difficulty. 'You said I haven't had to live with regret, guilt or shame but I will, for that. I'm sorry I hurt you, Millie. I'm sorry I made you feel worthless when you are anything but.'

He took a step back and gave a short nod. 'Have a good flight.'

CHAPTER TWELVE

IN CONTRAST TO the heat and bright colours of the Indian Ocean, London at the beginning of December was cold and grey, although the twinkling lights strung between lampposts and the Christmassy shop windows did give the illusion of festive bonhomie.

On my return I used up the rest of my leave methodically going through the hundreds of emails clogging up my inbox and the messages I'd received via social media, which wasn't as traumatic as I'd once thought, and engaging the services of a house finder.

It was with some trepidation that I eventually went back to work and I had apologies and explanations prepared, but I needn't have worried. To my amazement and relief, my colleagues understood. No one had talked to the press. Every single one of them was happy for me and it was such a relief I was even able to laugh at the odd joke about me being able to buy the company and give myself a raise.

I went to a couple of parties with my flatmates, who were equally sanguine about my win, and whether it was because I'd had time to brace myself or because I felt so invincible after resisting Nick's considerable charms, I found it surprisingly easy to spot the sycophants.

Naturally, I hadn't heard from him in the fortnight I'd been back and that was fine. I'd left my dress behind, having changed into a more flight-appropriate outfit that was more than a little damp having been through a quick wash, but I wasn't expecting to see it again. I didn't need to know how he was doing any more than I needed to feel any guilt for the way I'd handled things. He was the one who'd pushed for something I was incapable of giving. He'd said he got it but he didn't, not really. He couldn't possibly understand my dread of letting someone close enough to destroy me. Or the gut-wrenching deep-seated knowledge that there was simply nothing about me that was worth loving, despite what he'd said.

Over and over again I told myself I'd had a lucky escape, and so had he, but of one thing I wasn't quite so certain. However much I tried to stop myself, I kept revisiting the points he'd made about my mother.

Could I have had it wrong all this time? was the main question that kept ricocheting around my head. Could she truly regret our estrangement? But if she genuinely didn't blame me for what happened, if her affair and the subsequent breakdown of their marriage really weren't my fault, she'd have done something about it, surely? Something more than the occasional call and the odd email and text.

But perhaps that *was* my fault, I was beginning to feel. When I thought about it honestly, her calls were more than occasional, and I never returned them. I told myself that I was simply too busy but that wasn't true, and I had no excuse for deleting the emails and texts without reading them or shutting down the conversation every time Seb attempted to broach the subject.

Why did I do that? Because I didn't want to think even worse of my father? But the truth of it was, he'd been as flawed as anyone, as Nick had pointed out, so perhaps I should never have put him on that pedestal in the first place. After all, there was only ever going to be one way off it. And maybe I'd always needed to cling onto the belief that I was guilty as justification for protecting myself and my fragile, vulnerable heart.

The trouble was, if I allowed myself to believe that Nick was right about that then I had to consider the fact that he might have been right about everything else he'd said. About me and who I was. I'd have to accept that I really was gritty and determined, resilient and optimistic. I'd have to believe I was worth as much as anyone else. I'd have to trust him. I'd have to lower my guard and put myself in his hands. In the hands of a man who said he'd loved me for years.

Which could never happen.

Because once he got to know the real me he'd soon realise I was unlovable, wouldn't he?

And yet...

He *did* know the real me. He knew me warts and all. He knew how I took my coffee. What my favourite drink was. He'd seen me at my worst— whether stumbling out of a club or on the point of dissolving into a puddle of misery—and hopefully at my best. And, ultimately, he hadn't been put off by any of it. He'd wanted me regardless of my many flaws.

As the scales began to fall from my eyes, I realised that he'd always been there for me. He'd defended me. At my father's funeral, even though I'd been too devastated to notice much, I'd noticed he'd stood close by. He'd looked out for me on numerous occasions and still was. Even at the height of our hostilities, he'd wanted to help me.

I'd wondered what it would be like to have

someone like him on my side, who believed in me, and I'd had that without even realising it.

And when I'd suspected the truth about my feelings for him, I'd been so terrified about what they might mean, I'd deliberately pushed him away.

But what was so bad about any of it? He was everything I'd dreamed of but never thought I could have. He was generous and tenacious, sexy and thoughtful, and apparently in love with me. Because of him, I'd discovered who I really was. I'd regained my confidence in my abilities. Instead of being petrified of the money, I was now excited about the plans I had for it. With the exception of a couple of understandable blips, I wasn't rash and reckless. I made good decisions.

But I didn't always have to take them on my own. And I didn't have to always be on my own. The truth of it was that I missed him more than I'd ever thought possible. Now I'd had a glimpse of what it was like to have someone to talk to and share things with, my return to solitude meant I was lonelier than ever. Drinks with colleagues and the odd party courtesy of my flatmates did little to alleviate it for more than a couple of hours and I was only so strong.

Despite trying to convince myself otherwise, keeping thoughts of Nick and the memories of our relationship, the good and the bad, out of my head was far harder than I'd anticipated. I'd catch a glimpse of a tall dark-haired man in a suit and my heart would leap and then plummet because of course it wouldn't be him. He was on Suza in the sunshine and warmth, kite-surfing and sailing, having put me out of his head with a resolve that I'd surely facilitated.

How could I have done that? How could I ever have told him that what he was feeling wasn't real? My arrogance had been breathtaking, my cruelty staggering. When I recalled the look on his face when I'd basically told him he didn't know the difference between lust and love my heart twisted in agony and shame.

The regret I'd felt over various things in my past was nothing compared to the regret I felt now, because with all the realisations raining down on me, the hardest, the most painful, was that I loved him too.

That was why he had the ability to hurt me so badly. Because I cared so much. He was the only person I wanted to talk about things with. The only person I wanted to keep close. When he'd ventured out into that storm the dread I'd felt had had nothing to do with me and my money and everything to do with losing him.

And of course I trusted him. Why else would I have put on that show for him in the shower room, exposing myself both literally and metaphorically? Trust was a choice, and it was a choice that deep down I suspected I'd made days ago. He hadn't once let me down and I knew in my gut that he never would.

I'd been so blind, so stupid, so fixed on my issues and doggedly pursuing a course of action that I'd thought would keep me safe. But all I'd succeeded in doing was throwing away the best thing that had ever happened to me.

What on earth had I been thinking? What had I done? Would he ever forgive me? And was there anything I could do to fix the catastrophic mistake I'd made?

Twenty-four hours later, I was back on Suza, waving James off as he sped away in his boat, only this time I had no luggage and a pretty good idea of the reception I was going to get.

With every step I took up the jetty and along the wide sandy path that led to the villa, my heart pounded that little bit harder and my stomach tightened with ever increasing knots. I hadn't told Nick I was coming. I hadn't wanted him to take himself off and go into hiding, which he'd be perfectly justified in doing. But I knew he was here. I'd got my brother to check.

The hot midday sun beat down on me from a

cloudless azure sky, though that wasn't the cause of the film of sweat that coated my skin. The gardens, the terrace and the beach bore no trace of the storm that had ravaged the island only a few weeks ago. The lawn and the flower pots were immaculate. The pool shimmered. The house, however, appeared to be closed up. The windows were shuttered. Everything was eerily quiet.

Nick could be out kite-surfing or sailing, of course, but what if he wasn't, in fact, here at all? I wondered suddenly as I glanced around for signs of activity and found none. What if Seb was wrong and my journey had been made in vain? How would I make amends for everything then?

Straightening my spine and lifting my chin, I fought back the doubt and swallowed down the nerves. I had a speech prepared and I would do everything possible to see that it was delivered. If I had to wait, for however long, then so be it. If Nick truly wasn't around I would track him down until I found him.

I knocked on the front door and waited, my heart in my throat as the seconds ticked silently by, but there was no response. So I tried the handle, and, when it yielded, opened the door. I paused only for a second to consider whether or not I'd be invading his privacy if I headed on in. Of course I would. But did I care? No.

I walked through the cool airy space, batting away the memories that were cascading into my head in order to concentrate on the goal. There was the console table, I noticed, an intense rush of heat infusing my body despite my determination to focus. There was the spot where I'd told him he was mistaking lust for love. The sitting room looked as untouched as it had been before, but the kitchen was a mess. Papers were strewn across the dining table and chairs stood awry. Empty wine bottles lined up on the island and dirty plates lay next to the sink.

But of Nick there was no sign.

Feeling strange and off balance, as though I were having an out-of-body experience, I climbed the stairs, my limbs seeming to function without my direction. I checked the rooms, and eventually found him passed out on his back in the room that I'd once occupied, my pink dress screwed up in a ball beside him.

At the sight of him, unshaven, drawn, haggard but still so gorgeous my heart ached, the numbness disappeared and every emotion I'd managed to keep at bay—the sorrow, the regret, the remorse, the love I'd denied for so long—started battering me on all sides. How could I ever have given him up? Now I was here, could I actually put things right?

Desperately hoping I could, I leaned down and gave him a shake. 'Nick.'

He grunted and swatted at my hand, so I did it again. Harder. *'Nick.'*

That provoked more of a reaction. A split second after I'd said his name his eyes opened and he looked at me for about two seconds before he grabbed me and pulled me down on top of him. He clamped one hand to the back of my neck and planted the other on the small of my back and kissed me until I was hot and dizzy. With a muffled groan, he rolled me over and ran a hand over me, which made me moan and wrap myself around him since I'd missed him and this so much, at which point he froze and reared back, evidently fully awake now.

'You,' he growled, extricating himself from me and leaping off the bed as if he'd been burned.

I ran a trembling hand through my hair, my heart hammering like a steam train, my breathing so laboured I was going dizzy. 'Me.'

'What the hell are you doing here, Amelia?'

So I was back to Amelia. That was understandable. But those kisses of his had been something else and they strengthened my resolve as much as they weakened my knees.

'I didn't think you'd answer my calls,' I said, getting up and tugging my clothes into place with fingers that were trembling as a result of his passionate embrace.

'So you thought you'd break into my home instead.'

'The door was unlocked.'

'What do you want?'

'To talk.'

'I think we've said all there is to say, don't you?'

The bitterness in his voice chilled me to the bone, but what had I expected?

'No. I don't,' I said heatedly. 'There is more. So much more.'

The look he threw me was dark, his brows snapping together. 'Are you pregnant?'

What? 'No.'

'So you made it to a pharmacy.'

Not exactly. I'd put it off and off and then it had been too late. At the time I hadn't understood why I'd dithered but I'd realised later that I must have subconsciously wanted to be for ever linked to him all along. Nature, on the other hand, had had other ideas. 'There turned out to be no need.'

'You must be delighted.'

'Yet I'm not.'

'I'm not up to these riddles,' he said tightly. 'My head aches. Please go away.'

He stalked to the door and held it open, but I ignored it. 'I've come a long way to see you,' I said, planting my feet more firmly to the floor.

'That's not my problem.'

'I called my mother. You were right about her. She doesn't blame me for anything. She'd told Seb that she was jealous of me when she was at her lowest and regretted it ever since. It was all in my head. And you were also right about my father. He was no saint. He had affairs too. I was labouring under a number of misapprehensions and for years I let this dictate my life, but I can see now that none of it had anything to do with me.'

'I couldn't be less interested.'

'In fact, you were right about everything.'

'Not everything.'

I took a deep breath, overwhelmed by the need to get the words out that were piling up in my head. 'I'm so sorry for how I reacted when you said you loved me. I wasn't ready to hear it. My response was shocking. The things I said were appalling. I'm devastated I hurt you. I was scared. I still am. You hit that nail on the head too. Everyone I care about leaves me. But that was no excuse.'

'I would never have left you.'

'I know that now,' I said, my chest tightening with pain and regret. 'I was blinded by the hangups that I've had for far too long. I couldn't see what was right in front of me. You've never let me down and I know you never will. I do trust you. I love you. I really really do. I think I have for years. That's why your attitude towards me hurt so much. Deep down, I've always envied my brother for his relationship with you. I've been so jealous of the blondes. I mean, one night you rescued me from a party and I actually wanted to scratch the eyes out of the one you were with. I know your habits. Your fears. I know you. And you know me. We belong together, Nick.'

'No,' he said flatly. 'We don't. I offered you everything and in return you destroyed me. You're a reminder of my weaknesses and I don't need that.'

'I'm so sorry.'

'There is nothing for you here, so please, just go.'

'I don't want to go.'

'And I don't want you to stay.'

Right.

Right.

I blew out a breath and nodded slowly even though inside I was falling apart at the realisation there was nothing I could say or do to change his mind. I'd ruined everything. I'd killed whatever he'd once felt for me. I'd been such a fool and I had no one but myself to blame.

On legs that were shaking like a leaf, my heart breaking, I made it to the door and past him, even though I so badly wanted to stop there, beg him for his forgiveness and—

'Wait.'

My heart stopped and then began to thunder. Hope surged. I whirled around. 'Yes?'

'You forgot your dress.'

He thrust it at me and I took it numbly. 'Thank you.'

As I stumbled downstairs, my throat tightened painfully and hot tears started to prick at my eyes. What was I going to do? How was I going to get over this? Somehow I managed to pull out my phone and pull up James' number. He couldn't have got very far. I hadn't been here very long. I'd hoped for a better outcome.

And then, at the bottom of the stairs, as my finger hovered over the small green button, I paused, my heart crashing against my ribs.

No.

This was wrong. I couldn't just leave. Not yet. I hadn't turned over every stone. Not by a long shot. What if Nick was just trying to protect himself the way he had done for years? Wasn't throwing up a shield of aloofness and detachment and keeping me at arm's length what he did? Could that be behind his stubborn resistance now?

I had to know the truth and, as the fearlessness that I'd lamented losing suddenly stormed back, I burned with a need that was fiery and unstoppable. So I dropped the phone back into my bag, spun on my heel and leapt back up the stairs, adrenalin powering along my veins while my heart thumped with hope and anticipation, only to come to an abrupt halt when he burst onto the landing and strode towards me.

'Just so as you know,' I said, needing to get the words out before he said or did something to prevent me, 'wherever you go, I will follow you. I will lay siege to you. I will not stop until you let me prove to you that I love you. I will fight for you ceaselessly and however long it takes, I will win.'

'Is that so?' he said, his eyes blazing with something that put a rocket beneath my pulse.

'It's a promise. I am gritty and determined, remember? You won't stand a chance. Your armour will be obliterated. Your weaponry will be demolished. You might as well give in now.'

'Too late,' he said, taking a step in my direction and scrambling my head with his proximity and his scent. 'I already have.'

I went still. My breath stuck in my lungs while my head spun. 'What?'

'I have no defences against you, Millie. Not any more. That feeble attempt at it upstairs proves it. I can't let you go again. I've been utterly miserable without you. I've been drinking too much in an attempt to forget you but it doesn't work. Nothing works. You're everywhere. In the house, in my head, in my heart. I've been so tormented I've taken to sleeping with your dress. My apology on the quayside was pathetically inadequate but the sentiment was right. You are not worthless. You mean everything to me. I will spend every day for the rest of my life proving it to you, if you'll let me.' He stopped and frowned. 'Are you about to start crying?'

'Yes,' I said with a sniff, my heart swelling with love and relief and joy. 'Sorry. I know how much you hate tears.'

He reached out and gently wiped my cheeks with his thumbs. 'This is the last time I make you cry, I promise. I love you.'

'And I love you.'

He drew me into his arms and kissed me then, long and slow and deep, and I knew in that moment, without the shadow of a doubt, that wherever in the world we might be, whatever we might be doing, together was where we belonged.

EPILOGUE

Five years later...

HAVING LEFT THE six research students in charge of the lab, I wandered down to the white sandy beach to where Nick was frolicking about in the warm turquoise water of the Indian Ocean.

He'd found me the island six months after we got married and it was everything I'd ever dreamed of. A coral cay of around six hectares, it was, amazingly and conveniently, only a hop, skip and a jump from Suza.

The lab had been built fifty years earlier and could accommodate up to thirty. When I'd taken over, it had been dilapidated, overwhelmed by vegetation, and unfit for human habitation at least, but in the intervening four years I'd made considerable progress. While working on my degree in marine biology, which I'd finished, I'd sought advice and recruited the best. The station was now on the list of all the major universities, Zurich included, the reef was bustling with life and the hawksbill turtle breeding programme was going from strength to strength.

Numerous charities had benefited from my lottery money over the years, and even my mother and brother had eventually been persuaded to accept some of it. But no one was more grateful for everything that had happened than me. I'd won things that money could never buy. Happiness. Contentment. Confidence. The love of my life and the family we'd created.

'Remember I once asked you where you saw yourself in five years' time?' I said, smiling as Nick emerged from the shallows, our four-year-old daughter hanging from one leg and our two-year-old son clinging to the other while my heart turned over as it did a dozen times a day.

'I remember,' he said, depositing our offspring on the sand and striding over to take me loosely in his arms. 'I think I said that I saw myself with you and our one or two children.'

'What's the verdict?'

'That the reality surpasses my wildest dreams, and you know how wild those can be.'

'I do.' Even after five years, the passion burned hotter than ever, the wicked glint that I could see beginning to light the depths of his eyes never very far away. 'So. I was thinking…'

His gaze dipped to my mouth and his eyes darkened, his expression filling with the intent that without fail made my heart skip a beat. 'You must have read my mind.'

'Not that,' I said with a grin. 'The children…'

'What about them?'

I gave my abdomen a light pat, then wound my arms around his neck, lifted my mouth to his ear and murmured, 'How would you feel about a third?'

* * * * *

If you got lost in the passion of
Stranded with My Forbidden Billionaire
then you'll love these other magical
Lucy King stories!

A Scandal Made in London
The Secrets She Must Tell
Invitation from the Venetian Billionaire
The Billionaire without Rules
Undone by Her Ultra-Rich Boss

Available now!